HORTEN'S

MIRACULOUS

MECHANISMS

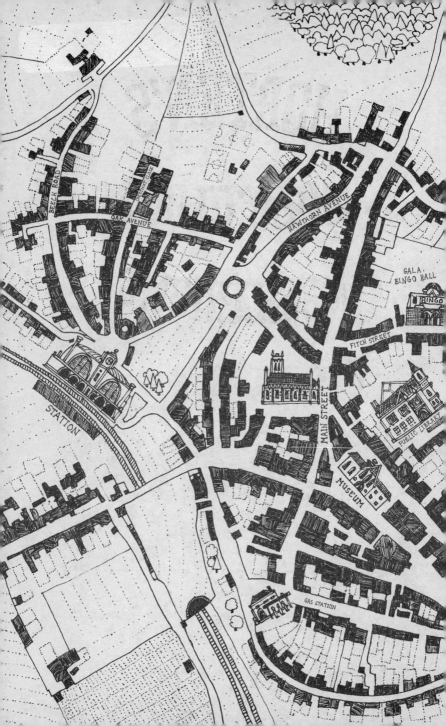

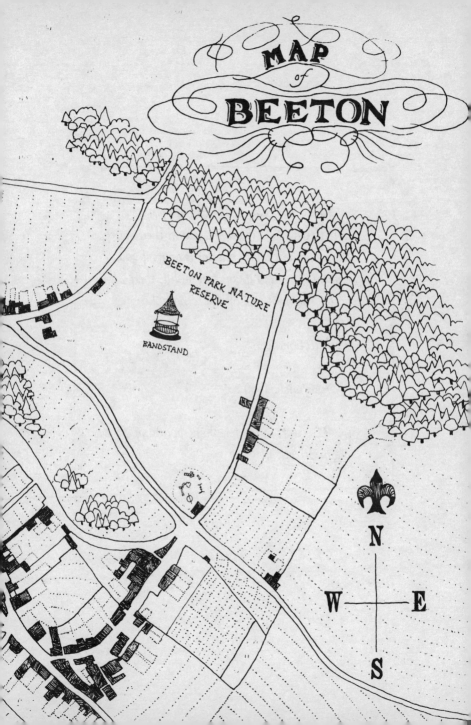

I have to go away, and I may not be able to get back. If I don't return, then my workshop and all it contains is yours if you can find it—and if you can find it, then you're the right sort of boy to have it.

Affectionately,

Your uncle Tony

P.S. Start in the telephone booth on Main Street.

HORTEN'S

MIRACULOUS

MECHANISMS

LISSA EVANS

SCHOLASTIC INC.

FOR MY GIRLS. –L.E.

Originally published in 2011 in Great Britain as *Small Change for Stuart*

ISBN 978-0-545-54164-0

12 11 10 9 8 7 6 5 4 3 2   13 14 15 16 17 18/0

Printed in the U.S.A.   40

First Scholastic printing, February 2013

CHAPTER 1

Stuart Horten was small for his age—the smallest boy in his grade at school—and both his parents were very tall, which meant that when he stood next to them he looked about the size of an ant.

As well as being tall and quite old (especially his father), his parents were extremely clever people. But clever people aren't always sensible. A sensible person would never give their child a name that could be written down as *S. Horten*. A sensible person would realize that anyone called S. Horten would instantly be nicknamed "Shorten," even by his friends. And Stuart had quite a lot of friends. He also had a bike with eight gears, a yard with a tree house and a large and muddy pond. Life was pretty good.

Anyway, this whole story—this unexpected, strange, dangerous story of Great-Uncle Tony's lost legacy—began when Stuart's mother was offered a new job. She was a doctor (not the sort who stitches up bleeding wounds but the sort who peers down a microscope) and the new job was in a hospital a hundred miles from home, which was too far for her to travel to every day.

"I could live there during the week," she said, "but I'd hate it. I'd miss you both too much."

So that was that, thought Stuart.

Life went on as normal for a day or two, and then Stuart's father, who was a writer (not of films or of bestselling books, but of difficult crosswords), came up with an awful suggestion.

"We could rent this house out for a year," he said quite casually to Stuart's mother, as if leaving the town in which Stuart had lived for his whole life was something quite minor. "We could move closer to your new hospital and see if we like it."

"*I* won't like it," said Stuart.

His father took out a road map of England and began to trace his finger northward. "Well I never," he said, his finger halting at a black smudge. He shook his head wonderingly. "I hadn't realized that the hospital was so close to Beeton. That's the town where I was born—I haven't been back in well over forty years. We could go and live there. It's quite pleasant."

"Oh, now that would be interesting for Stuart," said his mother.

"No, it wouldn't," said Stuart.

They didn't listen to him. At the end of the school year, they packed up and moved to Beeton, taking Stuart with them, and though they were clever people, being clever isn't the same as being sensible. A sensible person would know that if you *had* to move, then the worst possible time to move would be at the start of summer. Because when you arrived at the new house you wouldn't know any other children, and you'd have no chance to meet any until school started again in the autumn.

And—to make it worse—the new house (20 Beech Road) was small and boring and looked just like all the other houses on the street, and on the next street, and on the street after that. It was nowhere near a playground or a swimming pool. There was no front yard, and the backyard consisted of a square of grass surrounded by a fence that was slightly too high for Stuart to see over.

On the first day after the move, Stuart shoved his clothes and games into closets, and flattened out the giant cardboard boxes into which they'd been packed.

On the second day, there was nothing to do. Nothing, nothing, nothing.

Which is why, when his father said, "Ah, there you are. I was just thinking of going for a brief perambulation. Would you like to come too?" Stuart answered, "Oh, all right, then."

By "brief perambulation," his father meant

a short walk. That was the way he talked *all the time*, and he always spoke in a loud, clear voice, so that people in the street turned and stared at him.

Normally Stuart would rather have poured cold gravy over himself than go for a walk with his father. Instead, on this dullest of days he accompanied him out of the front door and went left along Beech Road, right along Oak Avenue, and left into Chestnut Close.

"When I was a youngster," his father told him as they walked, "there weren't any houses in this part of Beeton at all. This whole area was sylvan."

"What's *sylvan* mean?" asked Stuart.

"Wooded. And there was a stream running through the middle of it."

"Did you light fires?"

"Beg your pardon?" said his father, who was so much taller than Stuart that he sometimes had to bend almost in half in order to hear him.

Stuart raised his voice. "*Did you light fires? Did you dam the stream? Did you make a swing?*"

His father shook his head. "No," he said. "I was

never very keen on that sort of thing. I was too busy inventing crosswords."

They walked in silence along Hawthorn Avenue.

"Aha!" said his father as they passed an ancient red telephone booth and turned the corner into a street of shops. "Now, this is the older bit of the town. I seem to remember that the entrance to the family business used to be just along here."

He halted at a narrow passageway, but there was nothing to see apart from a pair of high-tech metal gates, firmly shut. "It's long gone, of course," said his father. "Though the name's still discernible." He pointed to a cast-iron arch that curved above the gates. A scattering of painted letters was just about visible.

"Horten's Miraculous Mechanisms," said Stuart after a lot of thought. He turned to his father. "What sort of mechanisms?"

"Locks and safes, originally, and then the business diversified into coin-operated machinery. Though by the time the factory was conflagrated by an incendiary I believe it was making armaments."

"By the time it was what by a what?"

"Burned down by a firebomb. In nineteen forty, during the Second World War, one fell on the factory when my father was away one night. My uncle Tony had been left in charge, but the fire took hold and the building was destroyed."

"Fifty years ago," said Stuart. "Almost exactly . . ."

Beside the steel gates were an intercom and a labeled buzzer that he had to stand on tiptoe to read: *Tricks of the Trade. Goods entrance.*

"So, what happened after the fire?" he asked.

His father, whose normal expression was one of mild happiness, looked suddenly serious, and he started walking again. It was a while before he spoke.

"It was all rather sad," he said. "I suppose it marked the end of the family. My father tried to start the business again, without success, and after a few years he moved away from Beeton. He blamed my uncle Tony for the fire, you see, because Tony had never really been interested in the factory at all, he was an ent—" Stuart's father stopped suddenly. "Good *lord*!" he said, staring ahead.

Stuart followed the direction of his gaze and saw a tall, shabby house, its yard overgrown, its windows boarded up, and its roof a patchwork of cracked and missing slates.

"That's Uncle Tony's house!" said his father. "The probate dispute must never have been resolved to the mutual satisfaction of the parties concerned."

Stuart ignored this last sentence. "What's an 'Ent'?" he asked. "You said he was an 'Ent.'"

"An entertainer," answered his father. "A prestidigitator."

"A what?"

"A magician. He used to do conjuring tricks on stage."

"A *magician*?" Stuart repeated. "You had an uncle who was a *magician*? But you never told me that."

"Oh, didn't I?" said his dad vaguely. "Well, I know very little about him. And I suppose it didn't occur to me that you'd be interested."

Stuart rolled his eyes in exasperation and walked up to the gate. It was encased in ivy, held tightly shut by the curling stems.

"Number six," he said, running his finger over the brass number that was half hidden by the leaves. "So, what sort of tricks did he do?"

"I'm not sure."

"And what was he like?"

"I don't remember him at all, I'm afraid. I was very young when he disappeared."

"He *disappeared*? What do you mean he disappeared?"

"I mean that he went away and never came back to Beeton."

"Oh." Stuart felt disappointed. For a second or two he'd imagined a puff of smoke and an empty stage and an audience gasping. "So, why's the house all wrecked, then?" he asked.

"Because there was a probate dispute."

"You said that, but what's *probate*?"

"The legal enforcement of the will. Uncle Tony left the house to his fiancée, but apparently they had an argument. She ran off after the fire and nobody could ever trace her. My goodness, it does look a mess."

Stuart stared at the front door. Several pieces of wood had been nailed right across it, but between them he could just glimpse an oval of stained glass, the multicolored pieces forming some sort of picture. A hat, was it? And a stick? And a word that he couldn't quite read?

"But I was in bed . . ." came his father's voice from the distance.

Stuart looked around. His father was walking away up the road, having failed to notice that Stuart hadn't moved.

"So, he left a present for me," explained Stuart's father to the empty patch of sidewalk next to him.

"Who did?" shouted Stuart, running to catch up.

"Your great-uncle Tony. He came to visit my house one Christmas Eve when I was a small child, but I was already asleep."

"And what was the present?"

"A box."

"What sort of box? A magic box?"

"No, a money box. I still have it, as a matter of fact—it's the one that I keep paper clips in."

CHAPTER 2

Stuart had seen the box almost every day of his life, though he'd never taken much notice of it. In the old house it had lived on his father's desk, and in the new one it sat on the windowsill of the study.

As soon as he got back from the walk, Stuart ran upstairs to get it. It was cylindrical and made of tin, painted with a pattern of red and blue interlocking rings, although half the paint had worn away so that crescents of bright metal showed between the colors. He flipped open the hinged lid, tipped out the paper clips, and looked into the empty tin. He didn't know what he'd expected to see, but there was nothing, just a blank, shiny interior. He slapped the lid back on again and stared at it for a moment. "Dad!" he shouted.

There was no answer. Stuart took the tin downstairs and found his father gazing out of the kitchen window with the kind of slack-jawed expression that he always wore when thinking up crossword clues.

"Dad, why did you say this was a money box?"

"I beg your pardon?"

"There's no slit in the lid. Money boxes have a slit in the lid to put the coins in. So why did you call it a money box? "

"Oh . . ." His father peered down at the tin as if he'd never seen it before. "I think it was written somewhere. On the side, perhaps?"

Stuart looked hard at the worn pattern and saw something that looked a tiny bit like a curly w. He turned the tin the other way up and the w became an м. But there were no letters after the м. He started to rotate the tin in his hands.

"Now that I remember . . ." began his father.

"It's not just upside down," said Stuart. "It's written back to front."

The o and the n of the word MONEY had completely worn away, but he could just about see the e and the y.

"Now that I remember," Mr. Horten repeated, "there'd been some kind of error in the manufacture of the box. The word MONEY was printed upside down and back to front."

"I just *said* that," said Stuart. "But I bet it wasn't a mistake." He put the lid back on again and weighed the tin in his hand. The bottom felt heavier than the top. "It's a trick box," he declared, with sudden certainty. "Great-Uncle Tony was a magician, and he gave you a puzzle to solve."

His father was gazing out of the window again.

"But unfortunately not a crossword puzzle," added Stuart under his breath. He upended the tin, and tried to unscrew the bottom. It wouldn't budge.

"Sorry?" said his father. "Did you just say something? I lost the thread . . ."

Stuart stopped what he was doing. The *thread*. It was a word with two meanings: not just a piece of cotton, but a spiral path, cut into metal.

Cautiously, he started to turn the bottom of the

tin the *other* way—and it opened in one smooth movement. He was so startled that he dropped both pieces, and suddenly there were coins all over the floor, gold coins (a sort of dull gold, anyway), bouncing all over the place. Stuart scrambled to pick them up.

"Good lord!" said his father, switching his attention from the window. "Where did those come from?"

"There was a little compartment in the bottom," Stuart told him. "They were packed so tightly that they didn't even rattle."

The coins were small with an irregular edge, a picture of a man with a beard on one side, and something that looked like a grid on the other.

"Are they worth thousands?"

"Let me see . . ." His father counted the coins into a little pile on the table. "Eight threepenny bits," he said. "A threepenny bit is worth just over a penny in new money, so they're worth—"

"Less than ten pence," said Stuart disgustedly.

"Well, actually," his father said, "they're no longer legal tender, which means that you can't spend them in the shops."

"So, they're worth *nothing*, then?"

Stuart flicked his finger at the little pile and it fell over. The top coin rolled off the table, onto the floor, and right out through the kitchen door, and he followed it, just to see how far it would go. Not far, as it turned out—only to the edge of the lawn. He knelt to pick it up.

"What's your name?" asked a voice behind him.

Stuart turned and saw a girl looking at him from the yard next door. She wore glittery hair clips and had a clever expression. She was resting her chin on the fence.

"What's your name?" she repeated.

"Stuart," he said.

"And how old are you?"

"Ten."

"So am I," she said, "but I'm a lot taller than you. A *lot*. What's your last name?"

He hated telling people his last name because of the whole "Shorten" thing. He shrugged. "Why do you want to know?"

"Because I do. I'm going to write an article about you and I need a full set of details. This is all I've got so far." She held up an open notebook over the fence so that he could read what she'd written:

New neighbors arrived Wednesday. Man looks like a giraffe, wears glasses, and hums all the time. Woman has awful hair, rides bicycle, and goes to work very early. One goldfish in small tank, looks dead. One son, probably about 8 years old.

"My goldfish isn't dead," said Stuart indignantly.

"I only wrote that it *looks* dead," the girl replied, underlining the word *looks* with one finger. "It's an impressions piece. But I need the true facts for tomorrow's edition."

"Tomorrow's edition of what?"

"Our newspaper. Me and my sisters are writing one as a summer project. April's the crime correspondent, May's the photographer, and I'm the general reporter. I just need your last name, the name of your goldfish, the name of your new school, the name of your old school, your date of birth, your favorite hobby, your favorite food, your favorite animal, your favorite sport, your shoe size, your exact weight and height . . ."

Stuart started to edge away from the fence half a step at a time.

". . . your best-ever Christmas present, your worst-ever Christmas present, your least favorite TV program, your most favorite TV program, your unhappiest memory, your . . . Come back!"

Stuart, who had edged almost as far as his own back door by this point, shook his head and dodged inside.

"Ah, there you are!" said his father as he entered. He was holding a Scrabble board. "I was just thinking of engaging in a little contest of—"

"Can I go for a bike ride?" asked Stuart quickly. "I'll be really careful. I won't go far. I won't talk to strangers. I'll wear my helmet. I'll be back in half an hour."

"Yes, all right," said his father, looking a little disappointed. "Where are you going to go?"

"Oh, nowhere in particular."

Which was a lie. Because Stuart went straight back to Great-Uncle Tony's house.

CHAPTER 3

Stuart locked his bike to a lamppost opposite the house and looked along the road. There was no one around. All the other houses on the street were small and modern and well-cared for, with tidy front yards and shining windows.

He crossed the road, glanced around one more time to check that no one was watching, and then he climbed over the gate.

The grass in the front yard was as high as his waist. He waded through it, stumbling over half-bricks and old bottles. When he reached the front door, he inspected the four planks of wood that were nailed across the frame. He pulled at one of them, but it held firm. He tried to peer through the mail slot, but it had been wired shut and he was too short to look through the stained-glass oval at the top of the door—though he could see the picture formed by the colored pieces clearly now: a top hat, a wand, and the initials T-T TH.

T-T TH.

Tony Horten. *Something-something* Tony Horten. *Terrifically talented?*

Stuart started to walk around the house, pausing to tug unsuccessfully at one of the boards that covered a side window. The backyard was even more overgrown than the front. There were swathes of giant stinging nettles and vast loops of brambles studded with unripe blackberries. Amid the jungle lay odd bits of junk.

The back door was large and solid and firmly locked. Stuart rattled at the handle for a while, and then knelt down to look through the keyhole. There was nothing to see but darkness. Disappointed, he straightened up. There was obviously no way of getting into Great-Uncle Tony's house. The excitement of the past few minutes seemed to dribble away, leaving him feeling flatter and sadder than ever. Without bothering to try any more windows, he carried on walking around the house, kicking at the litter in the grass.

As he reached the front yard again, his toe caught an empty plastic bottle and sent it sailing up and over the front wall. It bounced across the road and came to rest against the front wheel of a bicycle. A pink bicycle. A pink bicycle that was parked right next to his own. Standing beside it was the girl from next door. Glittery clips. Clever expression. She was holding a camera with a very long lens.

As Stuart gaped at her, she raised the camera and took a photo of him. "What are you doing?" he demanded.

She said nothing, but took another photo.

"Stop it!" he shouted.

The camera flashed again. "Anything to say to our readers?" the girl called, taking yet another picture. "Any comments as to why you're trespassing on private property?"

She was obviously nuts. The camera flashed once more.

Stuart turned and sprinted back around the house. Was there another way out? The wooden fence surrounding the yard was high, with no footholds, but right at the back, wedged into one corner, was an old barbecue grill, its white enamel lid blotched with rust. If he climbed up on that, he could probably get over into the next yard. Of course, he actually had to *get* to it first, without being first stung to death or shredded by thorns.

He looked across the sea of weeds. Just visible were odd little islands—discarded bits of furniture, an old trunk, a pile of boxes—which he could use as stepping-stones. He held his arms above his head, to guard against stinging nettles, and took a first, hesitant step onto a rotting armchair, its cushions furred with mold. From there he jumped onto a mushy pyramid of cardboard boxes and balanced briefly on what looked like an old gas meter before taking a huge step onto the lid of the trunk. The grill was only a couple of feet away now. But ahead of him there were no more stepping-stones, only a stretch of particularly lethal-looking nettles. He looked around quickly. There was no sign of the girl.

What he needed was a bridge. He retraced his steps and had just started to gather up some of the soggy boxes when he heard a beeping noise.

"Following subject into backyard of trespassed property," came the girl's voice from around the corner.

Stuart leaped from gas meter to trunk and started to lob the boxes ahead of him, stepping into one before placing the next. It took him four boxes to reach the grill, and then it was a simple job to scramble onto it and then up and over the fence into the neighbor's yard. He had no time to look where he was jumping.

In some ways he was lucky. He could have ended up in a pond, or gone through the roof of a greenhouse. Instead he landed up to his ankles in a compost heap. He climbed out and shook tea leaves and slimy bits of orange peel from his shoes.

A startled face looked through a window at him. Stuart waved cheerily and sprinted up the neat yard and along the side of the house, emerging onto the sidewalk.

His plan had worked! All he had to do now was

go around the block and stand watch until that awful girl went away on her bike. He walked up the road and turned right onto a street full of small shops. And stopped dead.

The girl was standing directly in front of him. Her face lit up. "Subject has just appeared on Main Street," she said into a walkie-talkie.

Stuart turned tail and began to run, but there were too many people on the sidewalk to allow a quick getaway. Instead he dodged into a post office and hid behind the door. The girl followed. As soon as she had her back to him, he hurried out onto the street again. And immediately he saw *the same girl*—glittery clips and clever expression—coming along the sidewalk toward him holding a walkie-talkie. For a moment Stuart thought he'd gone mad, totally mad, and then the words "identical twins" floated across his mind, and he realized that this second girl (unlike the first) was carrying a large, purple notepad.

She hadn't seen him yet.

He thought quickly. There was an old-fashioned telephone booth just outside the post office, and he pulled open the door and stepped inside.

It smelled repulsive. The floor was covered with mashed cigarette butts and horrible stains, and the windowpanes were encrusted with filth. The door closed softly behind him, and he crouched down to peer through one of the few clear patches in the glass. The second girl had now been joined by the first. They were standing together, scanning the sidewalks, searching for him.

All at once, he felt like an idiot. *Two girls*, he thought. *Here I am, in a stinking phone booth, and I'm hiding from two girls. I should just go out there and tell them to—*. And then, with sudden disbelief, he leaned forward and pressed his nose against the window. The two girls had been joined by a third, and they all looked *exactly* the same.

Identical *triplets*. He was being hunted by identical triplets. Stuart decided to stay put for a while.

A loud knocking made him jump, and he straightened up and turned. A woman was thumping on the door with the handle of her umbrella. "Are you making a call?" she shouted.

"Yes," he lied.

"Because there's a line, you know!"

Stuart felt around in his pockets for some money. He could always phone his father, he thought. After all, he'd been away for a bit longer than half an hour. His fingers found a single coin and pulled it out. It was the worthless threepenny bit. He turned it over in his hand a couple of times.

"Hurry up!" shouted the woman. "Either make a call or give someone else a chance."

"All right, all right," said Stuart. He lifted the receiver and stuck the coin in the slot, fully expecting it to jam halfway, but it clattered into the box. Now he had to remember his new telephone number. He paused, fingers hovering over the buttons. 0-2, was it? And then 0 . . . 3 . . . 4 . . .

He felt something brush his leg, and he looked down to see the telephone cord. It was hanging uselessly from the receiver, wires sticking out of the dangling end. Some previous visitor must have wrenched it right off.

"It's been vandalized," he called to the woman, holding up the end of the cable so that she could see it. She shook her head in disgust and walked off.

Stuart put the receiver back on the cradle and

jabbed the RETURN MONEY button a few times, but nothing happened.

He crouched down to look through the window at the triplets, and spotted them scurrying away in a tight little group.

Time to go, he thought.

And then the phone rang.

CHAPTER 4

It was impossible, of course. Stuart stared at the receiver, and then at the dangling cord. It swayed gently, the severed end nearly brushing the floor. And yet the phone was ringing.

Slowly, terribly slowly, he lifted the receiver.

"Hullo?" he said weakly.

"Is that a Mister Horten?"

"Yes," answered Stuart, so feebly that he could hardly hear his own voice.

"This is Beeton Public Library. We have the book."

"The what?"

"The book of photographs that you requested. It's in very poor condition, I'm afraid, so we can't allow you to take it off the premises. However, if you come to the information desk we'll let you study it. We're open between ten and five-thirty, Monday to Saturday."

"Thank you," said Stuart automatically, his voice a pathetic little croak.

The line went dead.

He rode home in a daze, and it wasn't until he had finished lunch that he managed to speak a single word, apart from "Yes," "No," or "Can I have ketchup with this?"

"Dad?" he said.

"Hmmmm?" His father raised his eyes from the book he was poring over. The book was actually volume seven of the *Oxford English Dictionary*, which covered words from *Hat* to *Intervacuum*.

"Could an electrical short make a phone ring even when the wire's cut?"

"Scientific phenomena would be more your mother's area," said his father. "However, I believe that given certain prevailing atmospheric conditions it would not be beyond the bounds of probability."

"Okay," said Stuart. "So that's a maybe. And . . . Dad?"

"Hmmmm?"

"Do you know where the library is in Beeton?"

"The library? It's ten minutes' walk from here."

"Can we go there this afternoon?"

His father, who had gone back to reading the dictionary, looked up again with a pleased expression. "Indubitably," he said.

"I bet that means yes," said Stuart.

There were two parts to the library. The old part had little turrets on the outside and a tiled entrance hall with a marble statue of a man reading a book, and the modern part had a glass staircase going up the middle and an enormous sculpture of a banana made out of wire.

"I'll just go and look at the children's section," said Stuart to his dad as they walked in together.

His father smiled and nodded. Actually Stuart could have said, "I'll just hang upside down from the wire banana and throw bags of flour at the librarians," and his father would still have smiled and nodded. Libraries sent him into a sort of trance, and he wandered off in the general direction of reference books. Stuart watched him go, and then went to find the information desk.

It was in the older part of the building, and the man behind the counter was quite old, too. He had long white hair, a rather severe expression, and glasses that hung on a chain around his neck. He was checking something in a card file, and he didn't look up or show any sign that he'd seen Stuart.

A minute ticked away, and then another. Stuart could feel his heart thudding.

"Can I help you?" asked the man suddenly.

Stuart swallowed. "My name's Horten," he said. "You called me about a book."

"Oh, so *you're* Mr. Horten," said the man, looking surprised. "Well, I must admit I expected someone older. Still, it's very pleasing to find a youngster interested in local history. I have the book here. Fascinating little volume—it was published in nineteen twenty-three, you know."

From behind the desk he took out a tiny

paperback with a faded pink cover and a cracked spine. It had very few pages.

"I ask you to take the utmost care when you study it," said the man. "It's our only copy and the binding is very fragile. No tracing or photocopying."

Stuart nodded.

"And you'll need to wear these, so as not to mark the pages." He held out a pair of white gloves, and Stuart took them, dubiously. "Oh, and could you sign this?" added the man. He slid a form across the desk. Paper-clipped to the top of it was a request slip. It was creased and yellowish. The name written on it in penciled capitals was HORTEN.

"My colleague found the card wedged right at the bottom of a drawer," the man told him. "It was under a whole pile of stuff, and I rang the number just on the off chance. If you hadn't answered, I'd have thrown it away. I was meaning to ask how long ago you requested it."

"Ages ago," said Stuart, the back of his neck feeling rather cold. "So long ago that I can't even remember doing it."

He took the book and sat down. It was called

Modern Beeton: A Photographic Record, and on each of the eight double pages there was a snapshot of the town.

The first picture was of Main Street. There was one car (looking like a shoe box on wheels), two horse-and-buggies, three bicycles, and lots of men in hats and women wearing gloves and narrow skirts. At the front of the picture, partly cut off by the frame, was a telephone booth.

Stuart peered at it. Not a telephone booth, he thought; *the* telephone booth—the very one in which he'd received the call. And there was someone in it. A small boy, his nose squashed up against the glass so that he looked like a pig. *The hustle-bustle of busy Main Street*, read the caption.

The next picture was of the interior of a train station, where there were yet more men in hats and women with gloves, as well as a great puff of steam bursting from the funnel of a train. In the background, just beside a large weighing machine, stood the small boy again, wearing long shorts and a jacket that was too big for him. His face was a little blurred, but it looked to Stuart as if he were sticking out his tongue at the camera. The caption read: *Beeton Railway Station. A thrilling hub of constant activity.*

Stuart turned the page. The third picture showed an outdoor swimming pool. (*Water frolics for the merry masses.*) This time all the women were wearing identical one-piece black swimsuits with thick straps over the shoulders—and so were all the men. The little boy was there again, dressed in the same clothes as before. He was standing next to the turnstile at the entrance to the pool and was holding his nose as if about to jump into the water.

Stuart continued turning the pages. A movie theater came next, followed by a gas station, a fairground, and a bandstand. The boy was visible in every photograph, although he was often a little blurry, as if he'd had to run to get into the picture. Stuart had the feeling that the boy had been following the photographer around.

Between the fairground and the bandstand there was a blank double page—blank, that is, apart from a line of print: *Ancient and modern together: a young man encounters the past.*

Above it on the paper were a couple of brown,

shiny marks. Stuart dabbed at them with a gloved finger and realized that they must be dried glue.

"Excuse me," he said, returning the book to the counter. "I think there's a photo missing."

The man looked closely at the marks on the page. "You're right." He frowned. "It's obviously fallen out somewhere. I'll make a note and we can check the shelving area and call you if we find it."

"My number's changed," said Stuart quickly, giving his new home phone number.

"And have you finished with the book?" asked the librarian.

"Yes, I suppose so." Stuart took off the gloves and handed them back. After all the weirdness and excitement of the phone call, the book had been a puzzling disappointment.

"School project, was it?" asked the man.

"No, it was a bit of"—he searched around for an answer—"family history."

"Horten," said the man, nodding. "A real local name. There've been Hortens in the Beeton area since records began."

"Oh, yes? " said Stuart politely.

"Blacksmiths, originally, and then locksmiths. Although in the mid-eighteenth century there was a politician in the family. You heard of Phineas Horten from East Nottinghamshire?"

Stuart shook his head.

"And then there was the Great Hortini, a Victorian entertainer whose real name was Horten. Heard of him? No? What about William Horten, the vicar who wrote the hymn 'By Eden's Bank I Walked a Mile'?"

Stuart shook his head yet again.

"Or, more recently, there was a magician who was beginning to get very famous when—"

"Tony Horten," said Stuart quickly.

"That's right," said the man, with approval. "You've done some research then, I see. Though he was generally known by his stage name. You're aware of it?"

Stuart shook his head.

The man smiled. "Teeny-Tiny," he said. "Teeny-Tiny Tony Horten."

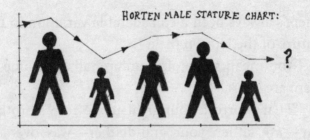

HORTEN MALE STATURE CHART:

CHAPTER 5

Stuart was so quiet on the way home from the library that even his father noticed. "Feeling indisposed?" Stuart's father asked.

"Mmm," said Stuart. Actually, he didn't know how he felt. It had been the oddest day of his entire life. He glanced up at his father. "What did Great-Uncle Tony look like?" he asked.

"Well, he was dark-haired, I believe, and brown-eyed . . . and . . . er"—Stuart's father hesitated for a moment—"not of exceptional stature."

"Do you mean he was really quite short?" said Stuart.

"Rather below average height, I think, yes.

There's always been a considerable variation in the stature of the Horten male."

"You mean some of them are tall and some of them are short."

"That's correct. Your great-uncle Tony's brother Ray—*my* father, your grandfather—was over six feet tall. Whereas *his* father—*my* grandfather, that is—was . . . er . . . not so tall."

"You mean he was really short too?"

"Yes."

"So being really short runs in the family?"

"There is certainly some truth in that statement."

"So you mean I could end up being as short as Great-Uncle Tony?" Stuart had always thought that when he reached the age of twelve or thirteen he'd start to shoot up. He'd just assumed it would happen. "Dad?" he pressed, when there was no reply. "Dad?"

There was more silence. And then for once, his father didn't use an enormously long word, but simply patted him on the shoulder and said, "You're a splendid chap, Stuart. We think the world of you." Which was kind, but which didn't really answer the question.

And when his mother got home (very late, as usual) Stuart asked her the same thing, and she got out a pencil and paper and medical textbooks, and gave him a twenty-five-minute lecture on the genetics of height. He didn't understand much of it, but he understood the answer, when it eventually came.

It was "Yes." Even though his mother was tall and his father was tall, it was possible that Stuart could end up as short as Great-Uncle Tony. *Teeny-Tiny* Great-Uncle Tony.

"And what are you going to do tomorrow?" asked his mother, trying to change the subject.

"Don't know," said Stuart.

The next day, he woke very early. He could hear his mother in the kitchen filling the tea kettle. He fell asleep again, and woke a second time to hear her softly closing the front door on her way to work. Everything went quiet for a moment. Then suddenly he heard the sound of running footsteps outside the house, followed by the snap of the mail slot and the slap of something landing on the mat.

He went downstairs. There was a flimsy newspaper lying on the floor of the hall. Right in the middle of the front page was a huge picture of Stuart. It showed him climbing over the gate of Great-Uncle Tony's house, a furtive expression on his face. He stared down at it, horrified, and then slowly, slowly, he picked up the paper and began to read.

THE BEECH ROAD GUARDIAN
Special crime edition!!

New Neighbors

Number 20 Beech Road has seen the arrival of the Horten family. Extensive research has revealed Mrs. Horten to be a doctor, Mr. Horten to be someone who sits around reading things, and their son, Stuart Horten (10, but looks younger), to be a potential BURGLAR! Yes! A BURGLAR! Or a VANDAL! Only one day after moving into the neighborhood he was observed trying to break into a house on Filbert Way, and only the prompt action of our reporter prevented a MAJOR CRIME.

Read full story on page 2!!!!!

Stuart turned to page two.

HOW I FOILED THE FILBERT WAY BREAK-IN
By our photographic correspondent

It was a warm day and I had just taken a pleasant bike ride around the block, when I happened to glance at a derelict house on Filbert Way. Imagine my surprise when I recognized my new neighbor, Stuart Horten (10, but looks younger), climbing over the

gate, obviously up to no good.
He then tried to break through
a side window, before—

Stuart couldn't face reading any more. The article took up the whole of page two. Page three contained some unflattering photographs of his family, taken on the day they moved in.

Page four (the back page) was titled *"Other News,"* and was obviously copied from the local paper, as it was dull stuff about construction work and trash-emptying days. At the bottom was a small picture, captioned *Our ever-ready staff. April, May, and June Kingley.* Three identical, clever-looking faces stared up at him. Actually, they were not quite identical. One of them (was it April?) was wearing glasses.

There was a noise from upstairs—his father's bedroom door opening—and Stuart hurriedly crumpled the newspaper into a ball. By the time his dad arrived in the kitchen, the paper was right at the bottom of the bin and Stuart was sitting eating a bowl of cornflakes.

"Ah, fully conscious, I see," said his father. "Any plans for today?"

"Not really," said Stuart.

"Another trip to the library?"

"Not yet, thanks," said Stuart.

"Or how about the Beeton Museum? I was looking at a leaflet in the library."

"I don't think so," said Stuart.

"It's quite a good one, I understand," his father told him. "With a collection of special interest for the numismatologist."

Perhaps, thought Stuart, he ought to tattoo a question mark on his forehead and just point to it whenever his father spoke. "For the *what*?"

"For the coin collector."

"Oh," said Stuart. He thought suddenly of yesterday, of the coin that he'd put into the phone booth, of the phone mysteriously ringing, and all at once he knew exactly what his plans were for the day. He looked around and saw the other threepenny bits sitting in a neat pile on the windowsill.

"Dad?" he said. "Can I go for a bike ride?"

CHAPTER 6

He rode straight to the phone booth. As he locked up his bike he could feel himself getting nervous, his heart pounding, his breath shallow. *Would it happen a second time? Could it be possible?*

There was no one inside the booth. Stuart pulled open the door and was hit by the awful smell again. Since yesterday someone had dropped a whole bag of french fries on the floor. He edged around the mess, waited until the door was closed and then took one of the threepenny bits from his pocket. It shone dully in the dim light.

"Okay," said Stuart. "Let's try it."

He reached for the phone receiver.

It wasn't there.

He looked around wildly. It wasn't anywhere. Someone had taken it.

And there was something odd, too, about the slot for the money. It was white rather than black. He peered at it closely and saw that it had been stuffed full of chewing gum.

Well, then, that was that. Glumly, he pocketed the threepence again and pushed open the door.

There seemed no point in going straight back to his horrible new home, next to his horrible new neighbors. He unlocked his bike and cycled slowly through the town. He passed a park with a playground and an old bandstand. The bandstand looked vaguely familiar. He glanced down a side street and saw a crowd of people waiting in line outside an old movie theater; that too reminded him of something. It wasn't until he saw the sign for the station that he realized he'd seen all of these places in the book of photographs in the library. The places were older now, and shabbier, but still recognizable.

He felt strange. He felt as if someone was trying

very hard to tell him something, but he couldn't quite catch the words. There was a bicycle rack outside the station, and he parked his bike. The main entrance was fenced off and displayed a sign saying DANGER! HARD HAT AREA, so Stuart followed an arrow around to the side of the building and entered through an arch beside the ticket office.

The interior of the station was a construction site. Green wooden panels blocked off most of the concourse, and behind them scaffolding reached as high as the glass roof. A thin film of dust covered everything, and there was a constant whine of power tools.

Every few feet, a poster had been stuck to the boards.

> **After one hundred and fifty years of grime, Beeton Station needs a cleanup. Please bear with us during the renovation project. We apologize for any inconvenience!**

Stuart pressed his eye to a tiny gap between two panels and saw a man in protective goggles cutting a block of stone. A fountain of sparks rose from the circular blade. Close by, another man was scouring the blackened bricks of the wall with a spinning disc. Slowly a rosy color was emerging from beneath the layers of soot.

Suddenly Stuart noticed an odd thing. Near the second man, on a part of the wall that was still dirty, there was one incredibly clean patch. The patch had a definite shape—a tall, thin rectangle topped with a large circle—and it was bright pink against the surrounding black, each brick looking perfectly new. Something must have been standing in front of that wall for a hundred years or more, protecting it from the smoke and dirt.

And he knew that shape.

It was the shape of the weighing machine in the photograph, the one that the little boy had been standing in front of. And he understood, somehow, that he had to find it.

He moved along the panels from one end to the other, squinting carefully through every gap, but there was no sign of the weighing machine. He opened a door marked NO ACCESS TO THE GENERAL PUBLIC and got shouted at by a worker. He ventured cautiously around the fencing sheets that obscured the main entrance and was shouted at by the same worker, who this time threatened to call the police.

It was just after that, as Stuart stood beside the bike rack wondering what to do next, that another man pushing a wheelbarrow full of splintered wood and chunks of plaster walked out of the blocked-off entrance and straight past him. Man and wheelbarrow disappeared behind a plywood screen at the end of the parking lot. There was a brief series of crashes, and then they reappeared. This time the wheelbarrow was empty.

Stuart waited until the parking lot was clear of people, and then ran for the wooden screen. Behind it was a large yellow dumpster, piled high with trash. A wide plank slanted up to it from the ground, and Stuart walked along it and peered over the edge. He saw the weighing machine right away. It was right in the center of the dumpster, leaning at an angle. Cautiously, he picked his way toward it, tiptoeing across broken boards that tipped and swayed beneath his feet.

There were three parts to the machine: a square platform at the bottom, just large enough for one person to stand on; a large round dial at the top, covered in glass; and a rectangular upright part linking the two. The whole thing had once been painted red, but over the years it had been scratched and written on, and the glass over the dial was cracked in several places.

On the base was a small plaque. It read:

HORTEN'S COMMERCIAL WEIGHING APPARATUS, PATENT JH25558

PLACE COIN IN SLOT AND STAND ON PLATFORM FOR A WEIGHT READING OF GUARANTEED ACCURACY.

Stuart took out a threepenny bit. This time he didn't hesitate, but pushed it straight in.

Nothing happened.

He looked at the instructions again: *Place coin*

in slot and stand on platform. Tentatively he put one foot and then the other on the slanted platform. There was a click, and the long needle swung slowly around the dial and halted beside a number.

79.

And just above the number, scratched onto the red-painted metal of the casing, two words were visible. Stuart craned to read them—craned and stretched and stood on tiptoe—and as he did so, there was an ominous groaning sound. The contents of the dumpster began to shift. All around him were cracking noises. Puffs of plaster dust filled the air. The weighing machine started to sink treacherously beneath his feet and rivulets of grit poured into the hole. Stuart clawed his way upward. For a brief moment he was on the same level as the dial, and the writing was close enough for him to read—it said GRAVEST FLATE—and then he had scrambled past it and was almost dancing across the moving surface, arms flailing, grabbing for the plank at the edge. He climbed onto it, breathing heavily, and looked back. Only the very top of the weighing machine was visible; the rest lay buried beneath the rubble.

Stuart sneezed and then sneezed again. He was covered in white dust, he realized, and his heart was beating wildly. He felt almost happy. And more than happy; *excited*.

The first threepence had shown him a book, and the second had given him a message:

GRAVEST FLATE. 79.

And now he just had to work out what on earth it meant.

CHAPTER 7

Stuart hurried home and wrote down the clue before he could forget it, and then he sat and stared at it for nearly half an hour.

GRAVEST FLATE.

79.

He looked up *gravest* in the dictionary, just to check that it meant "most serious." It did. He looked up the word *flate*. It wasn't in there.

He turned the piece of paper the wrong way up and looked at the letters upside down for a while. Then he realized that he was starting to feel hungry. He went to the fridge and made himself a cream-cheese, sliced-pickle, tomato-relish, and salt-and-vinegar potato-chip sandwich, which he ate while pacing around the kitchen.

GRAVEST FLATE.

"I used to love anagrams at your age," remarked his father, wandering into the room. "Did you know you can rearrange the letters of *Horten* to make the words *throne* and *hornet*?"

"No, I didn't," said Stuart.

"And your own first name," continued his father, "is an anagram of *Rattus*, which is, of course, the Latin for *rat*. And the word *Beeton*—"

"Why are you talking about anagrams?" asked Stuart.

"That piece of paper you left on the dining-room table," said his father, "I assumed it must be—"

Stuart was back in the dining room before his father could finish the sentence. If the clue was an anagram, then all he needed to do was rearrange the letters, and—hey, presto! (as Great-Uncle Tony might have said)—he'd have the answer.

He took a pencil, sat down, and began to think.

GRAVEST FLATE.

He rested his chin on his hands and thought

harder. The more intensely he stared at the letters, the larger they seemed to get.

Larger.

LARGE. All of a sudden he could see the word *LARGE.*

Feverishly, he began to rearrange the remaining letters.

FAV TEST.

No.

FAST VET.

No.

FAT VEST.

For a moment, he hesitated.

LARGE FAT VEST.

He shook his head. That couldn't be right. He turned the paper over and started again.

An hour later, he had a headache and six more anagrams:

A FLAG REST VET

A RAFT VET GELS

STAGE FLAT REV

FALTER GAS VET

LARVA FEST GET

and

GAVEL FART SET.

None of them made any sense at all.

"I think I might go for a moderately lengthy perambulation," said his father. "Would you care to accompany me?"

"No, thanks," said Stuart.

He heard his father's footsteps go out into the hall, stop for a second, and then return.

"An epistle for you," said his father, placing an envelope on the table.

Stuart frowned.

Typed on the front of the envelope was: S. HORTEN.

He waited until his father had left the house before he opened it.

```
Dear Mr. S. Horten,
    The special crime edition
of  the  Beech  Road  Guardian
has  been  causing  excitement
and discussion the length and
breadth of the Beech Road area.
```

"When are you going to write more about this serious and important story?" our readers have been asking us.

In response to popular demand, therefore, we would like to offer you, Mr. S. Horten, the chance to give your side of the story. Was there, in fact, an innocent reason for your attempt to smash your way into 9 Filbert Way?

In return for exclusive rights, we will print a special "Stuart Horten Says He's Innocent!" edition of the *Beech Road Guardian*, featuring a front-page interview with yourself and a voting slip for our readers to decide whether—

Stuart didn't bother reading any more. He crammed the letter back into the envelope, grabbed a red felt-tip pen, crossed out his own name, and wrote

NO, NOT IN A MILLION YEARS

in very large letters over the top of it. Then he turned over the envelope and scrawled

LEAVE ME ALONE

across the flap.

Snatching it from the table, he walked out of his house and right to the one next door. He shoved the envelope through the mail slot, retraced his steps, and found that his own front door had clicked shut behind him. He gave it a shove. It stayed shut. He was locked out.

He looked around. The road was empty, his father nowhere to be seen. In the upstairs window of the triplets' house a curtain moved and three identical faces peered down at him; they appeared to be smirking.

He felt like an idiot, a total idiot, and he wanted

to run as far and as fast as possible, but he forced himself to walk calmly and steadily away from the house. He even stuck his hands in his pockets and whistled a little, as if he'd decided on the spur of the moment to go for a stroll. He didn't think the sisters were fooled.

Once he'd reached the end of the road, he slowed to a dawdle. His father was likely to be away for an hour or more, so there was no point in hurrying. For a while he walked aimlessly, taking alternate lefts and rights, thinking all the time of his old house, his old friends, of all the ease and fun of his life before he'd come to this awful place. It wasn't until he took a left turn and found himself walking toward a brick wall that he started to pay attention.

It was a dead-end street, lined with old warehouses. A few cars were parked along the curb, but there were no people about. Somewhere a dog was barking, and curled in front of the brick wall at the end was a marmalade-colored cat. Stuart went over to stroke it, but it hissed at him and darted away. He watched it disappear along a narrow alleyway between two of the warehouses.

CRIBB'S PASSAGE, read a sign at the end of the alleyway, LEADING FROM POTTERS RD. TO GRAVE ST.

Stuart blinked, and read it again.

Leading from Potters Rd. to Grave St.

GRAVE STREET.

GRAVEST.

The clue wasn't an anagram; it was an address! He broke into a run, following the marmalade cat through the shadowy alley between the warehouses and emerged into a street of tall terraced houses. The cat was visible, sitting on the top step of a house with a red front door, and this time, as Stuart approached, it rose to greet him, rubbing its nose across his shins.

The number on the door of the house was *79*. Beside the door were two bells, the top one labeled TRICKS OF THE TRADE and the other FLAT E.

GRAVEST FLATE was actually *79 GRAVE ST. FLAT E.*

Slowly, very slowly, Stuart reached out his hand and pressed the bottom bell.

CHAPTER 8

He heard nothing from within the house: no ringing, no footsteps. After thirty seconds Stuart pressed the bell a second time and nothing happened again. He pondered for a moment and then tried the other bell. This time there was a very loud *bing-bong*. Still no one came. He rang it a couple more times and was just about to turn away when he heard hurrying footsteps.

The door crashed open to reveal a plump man in a nasty, shiny purple suit and silver shoes. He had a face like an eager hamster, and he was smiling widely.

"I'm sorry to keep you—oh." The smile dropped

as he looked down at Stuart. "I thought you'd be a client," he said. "You're not, are you?" he added.

Stuart shook his head.

"I didn't think so. Bit young. So, er . . . what do you want?"

"I'm visiting someone in Flat E. But the bell doesn't seem to work."

"Oh, doesn't it?" The man peered closely at the button and gave it a couple of jabs with his finger. "Well, I don't think many people visit Leonora, so she probably hasn't realized—I'll have to have a go at mending it. Come on in anyway. I'll give her a shout."

Stuart followed the man into the hallway. It was dark and thickly carpeted, and there were two closed doors at the end. The man banged on the left-hand door, called out, "Someone to see you, Leonora!" and then waited for a while, whistling an idle tune, one foot tapping in a relaxed sort of way.

"No reply," he said to Stuart, as if Stuart hadn't noticed. "She's probably harnessing the dog," he added, mystifyingly.

All of a sudden, a woman spoke from behind the other door. She said only one word—"Clifford!" and she didn't say it all that loudly, but the man leaped as if he'd been poked with a fork.

"Sorry, Jeannie, sorry sorry sorry—forgot what I was doing," he wailed, wrenching open the door and disappearing into a blaze of light.

Cautiously Stuart followed and found himself standing in the shadows at the back of a small stage. A couple of feet in front of him, in a pool of brilliant light, stood two little carts on wheels. Across them lay a long box, a bit like a coffin but dark blue and decorated with silver mathematical symbols. At one end of it, a woman's head—belonging to Jeannie, presumably—was sticking out of a hole, her long hair almost touching the floor, and at the other end there were two more holes through which her feet, in silver slippers, protruded. They were wiggling slightly, as if she were uncomfortable in the box.

"So, who was it?" asked Jeannie.

"Nobody," said Clifford.

"*Nobody?*"

"Just a boy visiting the downstairs flat. Shall I carry on with the trick? Are you ready?"

"Not quite," said Jeannie. "Just give me five minutes to finish icing this cake."

"What?"

"Of *course* I'm ready, Clifford. I've been lying in this box for fifteen minutes. Your audience would be gnawing off their own arms with boredom by now."

"All right then. Sorry." Clifford stooped and picked up two square pieces of metal the size of tea trays, each with a handle at the top. "*And now,*" he shouted in the direction of the audience, "a demonstration of mathematics. I take these twin blades of the finest tempered steel"—he clashed them together—"each of them sharpened to a deadly . . . Ooh, there it is again!" He looked up anxiously as a white dove swooped across the stage.

"Concentrate!" shouted Jeannie from the box. "You can worry about catching that bird later."

"Sorry. Okay." Clifford raised his voice again. "As I was saying, ladies and gentlemen, each of these blades is sharpened to a deadly degree of sharpness."

He drew a finger along one of the edges and then held it up to the light. Stuart could see a thin line of blood on the skin.

"So, let us begin our arithmetical journey. Long division!" shouted Clifford. He fitted one of the blades into a slit that ran across the center of the box, just where Jeannie's waist would be, and with a huge effort he slammed it downward.

"Addition!" shouted Clifford. He fitted the second blade just beside the first and shoved that down too.

"Subtraction!" He gripped the blade handles, one in each hand, and then with a sudden, dramatic gesture pulled the two halves of the box apart. The little carts rolled across the stage in opposite directions. Stuart gasped.

"And finally, we have multi—"

"Clifford!" screamed Jeannie. "My feet, get my *feet*!"

The cart containing her bottom half had started to roll down the gently sloping stage toward the audience. Clifford ran after it, made a dive, and just managed to grab one of the wheels. The cart jerked to a halt, and the box slid off the end, hitting the floor with a huge crash. Jeannie's feet, now pointing straight at the ceiling, carried on wiggling. Clifford buried his face in his hands.

"House lights on," said Jeannie, her voice like an icy blast.

Clifford trudged to the side of the stage and there was a thud and a click. The white spotlight dimmed, and suddenly Stuart could see the audience. Except that there wasn't one, only three rows of empty tip-up seats in a mini-auditorium, the red plush upholstery looking rather shabby and tired.

"Shall I get you out?" asked Clifford.

"No, please," said Jeannie. "I'm having the most tremendous fun. Come back in a couple of hours."

Clifford walked over to her. He pulled out the blade from the end of the box and lifted the lid. She wasn't cut in half at all, but was lying curled up, her knees bent to one side, her feet tucked up under her body.

Startled, Stuart looked back at the still-moving feet sticking out of the other end of the box. Battery-powered fakes, he thought. Simple, but clever.

"I've failed Grade Two Basic Magic Skills again, haven't I?" asked Clifford gloomily.

"Yes," said Jeannie. "But you can retake the course for the usual fee." She had climbed out of the box and was grimacing and rubbing her calves. "Why is there a small child watching us?" she asked.

"He's the one who came to see Leonora," said Clifford.

"Hello," Stuart called politely.

Jeannie ignored him. "Tidy up the stage then," she instructed Clifford.

As Stuart stood there rather awkwardly, wondering what to do, he felt a nudge on the back of his leg. He turned to see an old lady and a guide dog. The lady had pure white hair, drawn back into a bun, and a gentle, rather humorous face, and the dog was black and extremely hairy. Its nose was sniffing Stuart's knees with some interest—at least, he hoped it was the nose.

"Is somebody looking for me?" asked the lady.

"Yes," said Stuart, a bit uncomfortably. He had never talked to a blind person before. "I am, I think.'"

She shifted her gaze downward. "That's the voice of a very young man indeed," she said, holding out her hand to shake. "I'm Leonora Vickers."

"And I'm Stuart Horten."

"Did you say Horten?" asked Leonora.

"Did you say *Horten*?" repeated another, sharper, voice. It was Jeannie, rapidly crossing the stage toward him. "Horten, as in Tony Horten?" she asked. "As in Teeny-Tiny Tony Horten?"

"Yes," Stuart confirmed. "He was my great-uncle."

Jeannie stared down at him. Her expression was very strange: curiosity, and a sort of hunger. "I didn't know Tony had any family left in Beeton," she said.

"We've only just moved back here," said Stuart.

"And what do you know about your great-uncle?"

"Nothing, really." Jeannie's gaze made him uncomfortable. "Just that he was a magician. I've never even seen a picture of him."

"Oh, haven't you?" asked Jeannie. "My goodness, we must do something about that. Come along with me and have a chat."

It sounded more like an order than a request, but

Stuart hesitated, glancing at Leonora. The writing on the weighing machine had said FLAT E.

"But I came to talk to this lady," he said.

"Did you?" Jeannie cocked her head curiously. "Why? How?"

Stuart opened his mouth and then closed it again. His mind was blank. He couldn't think of a convincing lie, and he wasn't about to tell the truth.

It was actually Leonora who spoke next. "Because I invited him," she said. "I heard from a friend that the Horten family had come back to Beeton, and I thought it would be very nice to meet one of them."

Jeannie looked suspiciously from Stuart to Leonora and back again. "All right then," she said, "let's all go for a chat *together*." And placing her hand on Stuart's shoulder, she marched him across to the front of the stage and down some steps to the auditorium.

CHAPTER 9

Stuart looked around to check that Leonora and the dog were following. They were, Leonora moving slowly but confidently, one hand gripping the dog's harness. Above them, the white dove flew in lazy circles.

"For goodness' sakes, *catch it*, Clifford!" shouted Jeannie over her shoulder, striding past the tip-up seats toward a door at the back. She opened it and Stuart stepped through into daylight, and gasped. They were in a huge greenhouse with a mosaic floor and a glass ceiling that extended all the way from the roof of number seventy-nine to the roof of a warehouse directly behind. There was a fountain in the center, palm trees that reached almost to the glass above, and large green copper sculptures of lizards and butterflies. But there was also a row of buckets on the floor to catch drips from the ceiling, the fountain was a feeble trickle, and the mosaic floor was chipped and grimy.

"It's enormous," said Stuart.

"There used to be hummingbirds here," said Leonora. "I'd put sugar in my palms and hold them up, and I could hear the whir of their wings as they came to eat."

"Yes, it's not what it was," replied Jeannie bitterly. "We built it to entertain clients, but cheap foreign imports have cut our business right in half. Nobody wants quality magic any more. And the overheads are appalling." She steered Stuart past a peeling wrought-iron bench, toward a huge set of doors in the warehouse wall.

Across them, in curly script, was painted:

Tricks of the Trade

There was a smaller door cut into one of the large doors. Leonora opened it and marched Stuart through. If he'd thought the greenhouse was big—well, this warehouse was on a different scale altogether. He could hardly see to the other end. Row after row of shelves stretched away into the distance, but most of them were empty. Three forklift trucks were parked off to one side; there was only one in use, slowly ferrying a box labeled MAGIC CABINET along one of the aisles.

At the far end was a workshop. Stuart could see the flash of a welding torch and hear the distant *tunk-tunkity-tunk* of hammer on metal.

"This used to be so busy," said Leonora, her voice echoing in the vastness.

"Yes, all right, all right, Leonora," Jeannie snapped irritably. "There's no need to rub it in." She headed for a small, glass-walled office in one corner. Once they had all filed in, she closed the door, and the noise of hammering was muffled.

Leonora felt her way to a straight-backed chair and sat down, and the dog collapsed onto the floor beside her, looking instantly like a discarded rug.

The room was furnished simply, with desks and chairs and, in one corner, something that looked like a museum cabinet.

"Come and see your uncle," said Jeannie, tapping her long nails on the glass.

Stuart went over. By standing on tiptoe, he could just see a photograph. It showed a smartly dressed, very short young man grinning keenly outside a theater. Next to him was a young woman in a glittery costume, and she was smiling and pointing to a sign that read:

BOOK NOW!!
TEENY-TINY
TONY HORTEN
MINI MASTER OF MAGIC.
**Coming here soon
with his newest,
greatest illusion:**
THE WELL OF WISHES

"What was the Well of Wishes?" asked Stuart.

Jeannie gave a little jump. "And why would you

want to know that?" she asked, leaning over so that her face was rather too close to Stuart's.

He took a step back. "Just curious, I suppose," he said.

"So, you're the curious type, are you? Always wanting to find things out, and root around and search and probe and question and discover?"

There was a pause while Stuart tried to think of an answer. "-ish," he said.

Jeannie straightened up again. "The Well of Wishes was an illusion that was destroyed in the Horten factory fire before it was ever seen on stage. Do you know about the fire?"

Stuart nodded.

"Your great-uncle's workshop was in that factory," continued Jeannie. "It was where he developed and perfected his tricks, and after the fire there was nothing left of it except white-hot ash and clots of molten metal."

There was a sudden movement behind them, and Stuart looked around to see Leonora crouched over her dog, fondling its ears, her face hidden.

"And then he disappeared?" asked Stuart.

"Not until four years later. Although you could say he disappeared from public view, except for occasional performances. When he *did* give a show it was brilliant. Breathtaking. My father took me to see one when I was a very little girl, and I've never forgotten it. The Pharaoh's Cabinet. The Reappearing Rose Bower. The Book of Peril."

Her eyes were shining, her hard face somehow softened. "It was marvelous. *Marvelous*."

"And then what happened?" asked Stuart.

She shrugged. "He left. One day your uncle was in Beeton and then the next he wasn't. He walked out of his house and no one ever saw him again."

"So what happened to all those stage tricks—the cabinet and the book and the rose bower?"

"They must still be in his workshop. The one he used after the factory burned."

"And where is that workshop?"

Jeannie was very still, and when she spoke her voice was clear and quiet. "I don't know," she said. "It's never been found. Somewhere in Beeton there is a hidden room full of original and beautifully engineered illusions and I would give a great deal to find it. A great deal. I've searched, but I feel I'm missing . . . how can I put it? I'm missing a *key* of some kind."

She looked very hard at Stuart. "So, you've known nothing of this before? No little family stories, no bedtime tales about Great-Uncle Tony and the secret workshop?"

He shook his head. His father's last bedtime tale had been about Samuel Johnson and the compilation of the first English dictionary.

"Has anyone looked in the—" he began, and then there was a violent thud on the office ceiling directly above his head.

CHAPTER 10

The lightbulb jiggled on its wire, and Stuart cringed, expecting the ceiling to give way.

"*What* is going on?" asked Jeannie. She strode to the door and pulled it open. As she did so, there was a rattle of wings and the white dove fluttered past the office, landing on top of one of the forklift trucks parked a few feet away.

A second later, Clifford fell past the office window. "I'm fine," he called, scrambling to his feet and then wincing dramatically and clutching one leg. "Followed it onto the office roof," he gasped. "Very nearly got it. I was wondering if you'd count catching a dove as a grade-two skill. Ow."

He sat down on the floor again and Jeannie, looking extremely irritated, went out to help him.

"Stuart," said Leonora.

He turned to look at her.

"What else is in the cabinet, dear?"

"Um . . ." He went over and stood on tiptoe. "Besides the photograph, there's a little cage with a fake bird in it and there's a metal tube with Chinese letters all over it, and a—oh."

It was a cylindrical tin box, painted with red and blue interlocking circles. The word MONEY was visible, printed upside down and back to front.

"A money box," Stuart told her rather breathlessly. It was exactly like his father's, which he'd found the threepences in.

"Will you bring the items to me?" asked Leonora. The cabinet wasn't locked, so Stuart gathered up the bits and pieces and brought them over to her. She took them eagerly and arranged them on the desk beside her.

"These were some of the first tricks your uncle ever engineered," she said. "He was terribly proud of them."

"You *knew* him?" asked Stuart.

"Tremendously well. He was engaged to my elder sister, Lily—she was his assistant, you saw her in the photograph. Now take a look at this."

Confidently, she picked up the little birdcage. It was made of silvery metal, and the white bird within was of folded paper. Leonora moved her hands very slightly—and suddenly the cage was gone. Gone completely.

Stuart stared.

"It's here," said Leonora, pulling what looked like an umbrella spoke from her sleeve. She placed a finger at either end and pushed gently. The birdcage unfolded, the little paper bird spun on his perch and Leonora laughed. "I'll bet you're looking startled," she said in her pleasant, husky voice.

"And this is the Fiendish Finger Trap," she said, laying a hand on the slender silver tube. "The more you try to free yourself, the firmer you stick. Next to it is the Magical Money Box." It rattled as she turned it upside down.

"You unscrew the bottom counterclockwise," said Stuart quickly, and Leonora smiled.

"You must have seen one before. I know that the factory sold thousands." She twisted off the base and a penny coin fell out. "But have you seen the other trick to it?" she added.

Stupidly, he shook his head before remembering that she was blind. "No," he said.

She turned the money box the right way up again and opened the hinged lid at the top. "I wonder whether the penny coin will work," she said. "This old model was actually designed for threepenny bits."

She inserted the edge of the coin into a slit just below the hinge, and gave a little push and a twist. There was a springy click. With the lid still open, she turned the tin upside down again and gave it a shake, and a metal disk clattered onto the table.

"A false bottom," said Leonora. "Is there anything beneath it?"

Stuart peered into the money box.

"A circle of cardboard with the word *surprise!* written on it," he told her.

Leonora laughed, and then leaned toward him. "What's Jeannie doing?" she asked under her breath.

Stuart looked around. "She's fetched a first-aid kit and she's put a sort of elastic sock on Clifford's foot. He's trying to stand up."

"We don't have long to talk, then," said Leonora. "And I'd love to know how you tracked me down. I'm sorry I lied to Jeannie about inviting you here, but I could sense you were struggling for an answer."

"I was a bit." Stuart paused. "I'm not sure you'll believe it when I tell you," he said.

"I think you'd be surprised what I'd believe," said Leonora quietly. "Could you meet me the day after tomorrow? Eleven o'clock in the Gala Bingo Hall on Fitch Street? I go there every Thursday morning."

Stuart did the nodding thing again, before remembering to speak. "Yes," he said. "I'm sure my dad will let—" and then he realized suddenly that he had left his house *ages* ago, and that his father would be coming back from his walk to find Stuart gone and no note of explanation. "I'd better go," he said. "I'll be there on Thursday. I promise."

He hurried out of the office and nearly bumped into Jeannie. "I've got to get home," he said.

"Not before you tell me what you were going

to say before Clifford decided to jump without a parachute. We were talking about your great-uncle's workshop and you said, 'Has anyone looked in the—'" She raised an eyebrow.

"I was going to say, *the burned-out factory*," said Stuart. "Maybe he rebuilt it in the ruins of Horten's Miraculous Mechanisms."

There was silence, apart from the dove crooning from the rafters high above, and then Jeannie laughed. "No, he absolutely, definitely didn't do that," she said. "Something else was rebuilt from the ruins of the factory."

"What?" asked Stuart.

"This place." Jeannie spread her arms to indicate the enormous warehouse. "We're standing on the very spot. But in case you come up with any better ideas, let me give you this." She took a little silver card from her pocket. "My number's on it," she added. "And, Stuart"—she crouched to talk to him, in a way that made him feel like a toddler—"I really am the very first person you should speak to if you find out anything useful. Come straight to me. There might even be a lovely reward for you."

She smiled widely, but her eyes were like chips of glass. She showed Stuart out the back way, through the yard and the pair of metal gates that he'd seen on his first day in Beeton. After they'd clicked shut behind him, he glanced up at the lettering on the arch.

He thought of a fire so fierce that it left nothing but molten scraps, and then he set off at a run for home.

He felt as if he'd been away for hours, but when he got back to Beech Road, he saw his father walking just ahead of him.

"Hi," said Stuart, breathlessly catching up to him.

"Oh, hello," said his father, looking pleased. "Been

on an excursion yourself, have you? Are you ready for your repast? I shall be preparing a Neapolitan speciality, with fungal and *caseous addenda*."

"No *caseous addenda* on mine, thanks," said Stuart. And while his father got on with making a mushroom and cheese pizza (no cheese for Stuart), he hurried upstairs to his room, grabbed the money box, unscrewed the base, and tipped out the six remaining threepenny bits onto his bed. Flipping open the lid at the top, he inserted one of the coins into the slit beneath the hinge and gave it a push. There was an immediate twanging noise. He turned the tin upside down again, and the false bottom fell onto the bed. Then he turned it the right way and peered in. And read the words:

TO MY NEPHEW

CHAPTER 11

For a moment Stuart seemed to stop breathing. Then he reached into the tin with shaking fingers and pried out a piece of yellowed card; it had been cut to exactly the right size, so it fitted snugly. On the other side of it was a message, written in penciled capitals. Stuart recognized the handwriting; he had seen it before, on the library request slip.

I have to go away, and I may not be able to get back. If I don't return, then my workshop and all it contains is yours if you can find it — and if you can find it, then you're the right sort of boy to have it.

Affectionately,
Your uncle Tony

P.S. Start in the telephone booth on Main Street.

Stuart sat on the bed and listened to the noises from the kitchen: the tap of the knife on the chopping board, the swish of the dishwasher, the drone of a radio program on the history of public libraries in England.

And as he listened, he suddenly realized something: the tin of threepenny bits, the secret message, this entire adventure had actually been meant for his *father*, but his father hadn't been the right sort of boy. His father hadn't been interested in dashing about having adventures, and the only clues he'd ever been good at were crossword clues. So for nearly fifty years Uncle Tony's trail had gone cold, until Stuart had stumbled across the phone booth, and then the weighing machine, and now it was *his* journey. And perhaps Uncle Tony wouldn't mind too much, just as long as the right sort of boy found the workshop in the end.

And he realized too, that he would never go to Jeannie with the information, however large the reward she offered. This wasn't about money; it was about an unfinished journey: a Horten family journey.

He sat and thought for a while, clinking the little pile of threepenny bits as he did so. Each coin, he felt sure, had to have a different destination—a slot of its own.

"Dad?" shouted Stuart through the open bedroom door.

There was no reply. Stuart went all the way down to the kitchen and found his father listening intently to the radio, his knife poised in midair, a bit of onion speared on the end.

"Dad," repeated Stuart. "What sort of things did they make in the Horten factory? I know you told me, but I've forgotten."

For a moment his father didn't move, and then, bizarrely, he began to recite a rhyme.

"If it swivels, clicks or locks,
You'll read *Horten's* on the box.

If coins go in and gifts come out,
It's made by Horten's; there's no doubt!"

"You know, I haven't thought of that in decades," he added happily. "They used to print it on the advertisements. In those days nearly every business in Beeton had a Horten's coin-operated mechanism on the premises."

"Thanks," said Stuart. He sprinted upstairs again, snatched a pencil and paper from his desk, and sat and concentrated, trying to remember all the subjects of the photographs that he'd seen in *Modern Beeton: A Photographic Record*.

MAIN STREET—phone booth
BANDSTAND
MOVIE THEATER
TRAIN STATION— weighing machine
FAIRGROUND
GAS STATION
OUTDOOR SWIMMING POOL
(ONE PHOTO MISSING)

Then he fetched the Ordnance Survey map of Beeton that his father had bought at a local shop and spread it out across the bed. He marked the movie theater he'd ridden past on his bike, and also the park where he'd seen the bandstand. There was a field on the western outskirts of the town that was labeled *Old Fairground*, and five different buildings marked with a tiny drawing of a gas pump, but he could see no sign whatsoever of an outdoor swimming pool.

"Any plans for tomorrow?" asked his father over their pizza supper.

"I thought I might begin a summer project," said Stuart casually. "Mapping the best bicycle routes in Beeton. If that's okay?"

"That sounds fascinating. Will you be approaching it from a schematic or a cartographic angle?"

"Both," said Stuart quickly, before his father could begin a discussion on the different methods of mapping. "And I'll start right after breakfast."

CHAPTER 12

Stuart's first stop the next day was the movie theater, but when he got there, he realized that:

a) It was closed until the afternoon.
b) It was no longer a movie theater. It was a bingo hall.
c) It was called the Gala.
d) It was on Fitch Street, which meant that . . .
e) It was the exact place where he'd be meeting Leonora tomorrow morning.

Therefore it could wait. In any case, according to the notice outside, "*Unaccompanied Children*" were "*Not Allowed In.*"

He pressed his nose against the window, but could see only a foyer with a swirly carpet and a shuttered box office. He got back on his bike and headed for the park.

It was quite large, with a kids' playground at one end and a grassy area at the other. The central portion was divided into a sweep of grass, with neat flower beds, and a large wild area—the Beeton Park Nature Reserve. Stuart peered through the chain-link fence but could see no interesting animals or birds; only a sludgy path through bulrushes and a cloud of midges.

The bandstand was in the middle of the grass area. It was octagonal, with eight posts holding up the roof and a twisting wrought-iron railing around the edge of the raised platform. There were still traces of gold and red paint near the top of the posts, but the whole thing looked neglected and rusty. A large, weather-beaten bulletin board was fixed to the brickwork of the base, over which someone had stuck a poster advertising the Beeton Summer Festival.

Stuart went up the steps to the empty platform.

There was nothing at all to see, apart from a few cigarette butts and a dented Coke can. He didn't know what he'd expected, but he'd expected *something*—perhaps a machine (made in the Horten factory) that played a selection of brass-band tunes on insertion of a threepence. Feeling frustrated, he went back to where he'd left his bike, and took a moment to consult the map.

Next stop, the old fairground.

It took him ages to find it. That was because he'd been looking for a field. He'd imagined stumbling across a broken merry-go-round, all covered in ivy. What he found instead was a brand-new housing complex with a gate across the entrance and a bored-looking salesman sitting in a trailer next to it.

"Thinking of buying something, Sonny?" he asked Stuart sarcastically. "Here, take a leaflet."

Stuart glanced at the cover.

CAROUSEL PROPERTIES
Exclusive homes at affordable prices.
We won't be taking you for a ride.

"No, thank you," Stuart said. He turned away, and then had a thought. "Before the new houses were built," he asked, "was there anything here? Anything left over from when it was a fairground?"

The salesman shrugged. "Search me," he said. "You don't think I live in this dump, do you? I drive over from Birmingham every day."

Stuart got back on his bike. *Gas stations next*, he thought.

The first two were modern, the third had been converted into apartments, and the fourth demolished. The fifth, however, was empty and weed covered, with cracked pumps and a boarded-up store. Stuart walked all the way around the building. On one of the building's side walls, some faded lettering was just about visible: BICYCLE REPAIRS. Below it on the ground were four shallow holes in the cement, as if something had once been fixed there.

Stuart walked around the building a second time, and found nothing more. He sat on a wall and ate the interesting bits of his packed lunch, and then, feeling grim but determined, he biked back to the park.

The bandstand was no more inspiring the second time, and there wasn't a trace of a clue. Stuart leaned his elbows on the railing and looked out across Beeton Park. The playground was full of children, but the stretch of grass was almost empty, apart from a couple of dogs racing in circles. On the far side a man with a pair of binoculars was opening the gate into the nature reserve.

Stuart closed his eyes and tried to think. *Did I miss something? Something tiny and subtle? Something huge and blindingly obvious?*

He opened his eyes again. After a moment, he frowned. Over by the nature reserve there were now six men with binoculars lining up to go through the gate, and another nine or ten hurrying to catch up with them. Curious, Stuart left the bandstand and walked over. All the men were wearing raincoats and carrying cameras and notebooks, and they seemed strangely excited about something. The last of them was going through the gate into the reserve just as

Stuart arrived; he was shorter than the others.

"Excuse me, what's happening in there?" Stuart called out.

The man turned around, and Stuart saw that it was actually a tall boy, not much older than himself.

"We've had a rarity alert," said the boy. "A single specimen of *Ixobrychus minutus.*"

"A what?" asked Stuart; it was like talking to his father.

"A little bittern," said the boy.

"Is that a bird?"

The boy looked at Stuart in amazement. "Of course it's a *bird*!" he replied contemptuously. "It's a bird of reed bed and swamp. Hence its appearance here."

"This isn't a swamp," said Stuart a bit crossly; he'd had an irritating sort of day, and now this boy was treating him like an idiot.

"As a matter of fact, it is," said the boy. "The definition of *swamp* is an area of poor drainage. There used to be an outdoor swimming pool here, and when it was filled in, it created perfect swamp conditions. Only four little bitterns were seen in this country last year, and two of them were right here. Anyway, I've got to go now. Good-bye."

He went through the gate, and disappeared along a path between the reeds. For a moment Stuart was too stunned to move, and then a great wave of excitement whooshed through him, and he hurried after the boy along the same path.

The reeds were very tall, and the tracks narrow and muddy. Stuart turned left and then right and then left again, and soon he no longer had any idea where the gate was. Every few minutes he'd stumble across a different group of men with binoculars. At the sound of his footsteps they'd turn to look at him accusingly, and he'd try to tiptoe past. So much mud had stuck to his sneakers that it looked as if he were wearing enormous brown slippers.

The first sign of the outdoor swimming pool he saw was the old diving board, blotched with mold. It reared above the rushes like a Diplodocus in a primeval forest. Soon after that, he spotted a wooden bulletin board, a few feet off the path. He struggled through the reeds toward it and read the faded lettering:

BEETON PARK
SWIMMING POOL

NO JUMPING
NO RUNNING
NO BALL GAMES

Right next to it was a bench, its wooden slats rotten with age.

". . . Of course, this isn't what you'd call an *official* nature reserve," said a voice from the path. "There's no restrictions whatsoever on who can visit, so schoolkids can just crash around all over the place, disturbing the wildlife. It's not surprising we can't find what we're looking for . . ."

Stuart quickly sat down on the edge of the bench, so that the passing group of bird-watchers couldn't see him. He felt a bit indignant; he'd hadn't crashed around at all, he'd been as quiet as a—

There was a sudden weird barking noise just to his left. He turned his head and saw a bird perching on a dead branch. It had an orange bill and black wings, and it looked him straight in the eye before making the noise again. It sounded like a dog with laryngitis.

A stampede of bird-watchers came back along the path, waving their binoculars excitedly. The bird called one more time, and then took to the air, flapping slowly away. The bird-watchers turned around again and stampeded after it.

Stuart was still staring at the branch that the bird—the little bittern—had been sitting on. It was a very odd branch, curved in a tight loop. He stood up and walked through the muddy undergrowth toward it. He reached out a hand and touched its rough, reddish surface. It wasn't dead wood; it was metal. He parted the tangle of stems that surrounded the object and realized that he was looking at a turnstile. It was rusting and crooked, and on one side of it was a small box, with a slot for a coin.

Slowly, he took another threepence from his pocket and placed it in the slot. Then he leaned against the rung of the turnstile and pushed. Nothing happened. He pushed harder. There was a horrible grating noise followed by the clatter of the coin dropping into the mechanism, and then the rung turned suddenly and Stuart shot through, tripped on a root, and fell flat on his face. He picked himself up—his jeans, his T-shirt, his entire body *covered* with mud—and looked back toward the turnstile. Nothing seemed to have changed.

He gave the rung another tug, but it didn't move. He looked at the slot and at the little box into which the money must have fallen. It looked different; one side was now sticking out slightly, like the edge of a door. He pried it open, reached inside for the threepence, and felt something that wasn't a coin.

He took out the object and stared at it.

It was a key. A large, heavy back-door key.

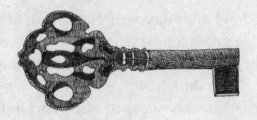

CHAPTER 13

He meant to go immediately to Uncle Tony's house—he meant to cycle there as fast as he possibly could, climb over the gate, and try that key in the lock—but as soon as he got out of the park, people began to point at him and laugh.

"Help! Help! It's the creature from the Planet Ooze!" called out a sniggering teenage girl, and it was clear that until he cleaned himself up, he was just too noticeable for secretive activities.

He biked home on the quietest streets he could find. He'd have a shower, he thought, and change his clothes, and then he could go right out again without everyone in Beeton noticing him.

The front door was open. He took off his shoes and made a dash for the stairs.

"Oh, *there* you are!" said his mother, opening the door from the kitchen.

"Hello!" He was surprised. She wasn't usually at home until halfway through the evening.

"We had a flood in the lab," she told him. "A pipe burst, so I thought I would take an afternoon off, for once."

"Aha!" said his father, looking over her shoulder. "I thought I could detect a somewhat mephitic odor, and now I can see its alluvial origin."

"I fell over in some smelly mud," said Stuart.

"Oh, so you did," acknowledged his mother, apparently noticing his head-to-foot sludge coating for the first time. "Anyway, we're expecting guests," she continued. "I was just thinking that it must be a bit lonely for you here in Beeton, and then I bumped into some children, exactly your age, right on this street, and I thought, seize the moment . . ."

Oh, no, thought Stuart. *Oh, no.*

". . . and I invited them around for tea."

The doorbell rang.

"And here they are!" said his mother.

She opened the front door—and there stood the Kingley triplets. Three sets of eyes gazed at Stuart. Three faces registered disgust and horror at his appearance. Three noses wrinkled at the smell.

"Hello, Stuart," said the one with glasses.

"I'll just go and get washed," he said, and fled up the stairs.

He took as long as he possibly could, but when his mother called up to him for the third time, Stuart knew he could avoid it no longer.

"Your guests are in the dining room," she said to him as he came down the stairs with incredible slowness. "I'm not going to bother you," she added. "I know there's nothing worse than parents interfering. I'll leave you alone to enjoy yourselves."

Stuart opened the door.

The triplets were sitting around the table. They looked at him in silence.

Avoiding their gaze, he sat down on the only empty chair. On the table was a plate of peanut-butter sandwiches, a plate of scones with jam and cream, a plate of chocolate brownies, and a plate of mini cupcakes. He took two of everything and began to eat.

One of the triplets tutted disapprovingly. "*Manners makyth man*," she said.

"What?" asked Stuart, his mouth full.

"It's a quote," she said. "It means you shouldn't speak with your mouth full, and you should offer food to guests before you start eating yourself."

Stuart shrugged. "You can die of starvation, for all I care. And if you're talking about manners, then what do you call following someone around and taking pictures of them and writing horrible things about them in a stupid newspaper?"

"We call it investigative journalism," said one of the triplets.

"I call it snooping," said Stuart.

"We at the *Beech Road Guardian*—" began a triplet.

"You at the *Nosy Parker Weekly*," interrupted Stuart, imitating her prissy little voice.

"Now you're being rude," said another triplet. "And if we're going to—"

The door opened, and they all stopped talking

and sat upright. Stuart's mom poked her head into the room. "Everyone having a good time?" she asked.

They all nodded. Mrs. Horten shut the door again.

"Now, where were we?" asked a triplet.

"I was being rude to you," said Stuart.

"No, you were being rude to *her*," said the triplet, nodding at one of her sisters.

Stuart shrugged again. "Can't see it makes any difference. You're all exactly the same."

"No, we're *not!*" screamed the girls.

The door opened again. "Still having a good time?" asked Stuart's mother. They all nodded. "I forgot to say," she added, "there was a phone call for you from the library, Stuart. They wanted to tell you that the missing photo from the book has turned up. Does that make sense?"

"Yes," said Stuart. "Thanks."

His mother closed the door again.

"We're nothing like each other," continued one of the triplets immediately. "June's hair has got a parting on the left, mine's got a parting on the right, and April has got *glasses*."

"Well, you all *sound* the same," said Stuart.

"Not when you get to know us."

"But I've already known you for *three months*," said Stuart. "Get it?" he added. "April, May, and June?"

"Oh, very funny," said April, the one with the glasses. "And if you're going to make jokes about names, then you'd better be careful, Mr. S. Horten. Bet you get called '*Shorty*.'"

"Bet you get called '*Speccy*,'" snapped Stuart. He could tell from her expression—a wince—that she did.

The door opened again. This time it was Stuart's father. "I'm here to take an order for potables," he said. "We have a wide choice of citrus cordials and also a gaseous syrup-based libation."

"Cola, please," said Stuart.

"Same for us, please," said June.

"I shall be back precipitately with your chosen beverages," announced his father, leaving the room.

There was a pause, and then May and June looked at each other and sniggered.

"He's weird!" said May.

Stuart took a breath and was about to say something really, truly, incredibly rude to her (because, although she was right that his dad was weird, it was still *his dad*) when April unexpectedly spoke up.

"It's not fair to laugh," she said sharply to her sisters. "No one can help their parents. What about when our mom sings? What about our dad's shorts that he wore to the school party last year, which had a hole in the butt? We hated it when people made fun of him."

May and June looked a tiny bit shamefaced.

"So, anyway," said April, turning to Stuart. "Why *were* you trying to break into that house?"

"Don't you ever give up?" asked Stuart. He'd just at that moment been beginning to think that perhaps April wasn't quite as bad as the other two.

She shook her head. "A good crime reporter never wastes an opportunity."

"Okay," he said tiredly. "My great-uncle Tony used to live there, so I was curious about it. I just wanted to look around." He sat back and folded his arms.

"That's it?" asked April.

"That's it."

"Simple curiosity?"

"Simple curiosity."

"I see." She reached into her pocket and took out a very small glittery notepad, and leafed back through the pages. "So at that point, were you already aware that the building in question was the subject of a demolition order?"

Stuart gaped at her. "*What*?" he managed to say.

"Your great-uncle's house is going to be knocked down," she said. "Didn't you know?"

CHAPTER 14

"What are you talking about?" asked Stuart. "What do you mean?"

"The land's been taken over by the local council," said April. "The house has been empty for more than forty years, so they're going to knock it down and put up a block of apartments instead."

"When?"

"Next week. Monday, I think."

"But how do you know?"

She shook her head. "A good journalist doesn't reveal her sources."

"You're ten," snapped Stuart. "You don't have any sources."

April flushed and tossed her head. "Well, as a matter of fact, I heard my dad tell a friend of his," she said.

"And how does your dad know?" asked Stuart.

"He's a builder," said all the triplets simultaneously.

At that point, Stuart's father came in with the drinks and said, "Behold, I bring hydration for your powwow," and May and June started giggling again and didn't stop until the dreadful tea party was over.

But Stuart barely noticed. He was too busy working out exactly when he could get back to Great-Uncle Tony's house. Because now he was running out of time.

That night, he set the alarm on his wristwatch for four a.m., and it was still beeping away madly when he eventually woke at ten past six. He hauled himself out of bed and looked through the window. His mother was just wheeling her bicycle up the drive, and he watched her cycle away along the road, orange helmet bobbing. Then he dressed quickly, hung the key on a piece of string around his neck, stuck two of the threepences in his pocket, just in case, and very quietly left the house. He had, he calculated, an hour and a half before his father woke up.

It took him only five minutes to get to Uncle Tony's house, whizzing along empty roads in the pale morning light, but when he turned the corner into the street, he braked hard. Work had already started. There was scaffolding up the side of the house and a front loader—empty as yet—squatting in the road outside.

Someone had unwired the front gate. Stuart pushed it open and waded through the dewy grass to the door. There were still planks nailed across it, but above them a sheet of paper in a plastic envelope had been stapled to the frame. It was too high up for him to read properly, but he could see the words DEMOLITION ORDER in large letters near the top.

There was still no one about. Quickly he made his way to the back of the house and lifted the key from around his neck. It slid smoothly into the keyhole and turned with a sharp click. He opened the door.

The first thing Stuart noticed was that it was very, very dark. He'd completely forgotten that all the windows were boarded up, and stupidly he hadn't thought to bring a flashlight.

He opened the back door as widely as possible and looked around. He was standing in a large square kitchen, lined with cupboards. He opened one of the cupboards at random and found a chipped mug and a box of matches. Unable to believe his luck, he shook the box and then looked inside: three matches, bent like bananas, lay within. He opened a few more cupboards, but found nothing except old dishes and dead flies, and then he tried under the sink, and unearthed the stub of an old candle.

The first match folded limply in half when he struck it, but the second produced a tiny, bluish flame. Holding his breath, Stuart held it to the wick. A clear yellow light grew and steadied. Cupping a hand around the flame, he closed the back door again and began to explore.

There were two doors out of the kitchen. The first led to a small cellar, festooned with cobwebs and empty except for a pile of coal. The second door opened into a passageway. Stuart walked along it cautiously, the candle flame dancing.

Through an arch to the left was a dining room, the table covered with what looked like a gray furry cloth. Stuart touched it, and his finger sunk to the knuckle. It wasn't a cloth, but a layer of dust as thick as a rug. He continued along the passage and through another arch into a long living room, the walls glinting with framed pictures, the furniture as dusty as the table had been.

He paused beside one of the pictures. It was a theater poster for the Nottingham Hippodrome, and at the top of the list of acts was Great-Uncle Tony's name, accompanied by a small black-and-white photograph. As Stuart peered up at his great-uncle's face—like a sparkier version of his own father's—the candle flame began to flicker wildly, and he realized that there was a draft swirling around his knees. He took a step back and saw a broad, empty fireplace, almost invisible in the shadows. He shielded the flame and moved on into the front hall.

In the trembling yellow light, Stuart explored room after room. In the downstairs study, he found a family of mice nesting in the ruined seat of a chair. In the bathroom he disturbed a bat, which flew in worried loops around his head. In one of the upstairs bedrooms he found a wardrobe full of moths and a drawer heaving with beetles.

At every turn, he expected to stumble upon something significant, but all he could find was wildlife. Admittedly, the beetles were fascinating, scrambling over one another as they panicked in the candlelight. Stuart stood staring at them for at least a minute before realizing that a low noise coming from outside the house was getting louder.

It was a truck, backing up. And there were shouts too, and boots on the pavement and the whine of the gate hinge. He went over to the window and tried to peer through a slit between the boards, but before he could see anything at all he heard a regular *thud, thud, thud* and realized that someone was climbing up the ladder onto the scaffolding.

And from downstairs, he could hear a ripping, tearing noise, as someone else started to pull the planks away from the front door.

Stuart blew out the candle and ran for it.

CHAPTER 15

Stuart hurtled down the stairs, just as sunlight flooded through the newly uncovered stained glass of the front door, illuminating the jaunty hat and wand and the letters T-T TH. The living room was still in darkness, and as he tried to hurry he found himself kicking a footstool halfway across the room. The crash sounded enormous, but by now there seemed to be crashes coming from all sides of the house.

He carried on groping his way toward the kitchen, but before he got there he heard a different sort of noise: quieter but distinct. It was the sound of the back door being opened.

"Here, it's not locked," said a man's voice, surprised.

Stuart stood paralyzed. If he was caught, he'd get into trouble. The builders might even tell the police, but they'd definitely, definitely tell his parents. If his mom and dad found out that he'd been trespassing on condemned property at seven in the morning, then they wouldn't trust him to go off by himself at all, and then that would be that—the whole quest smashed, the trail frozen. The threepences would rust unused, while somewhere in Beeton, Great-Uncle Tony's workshop would remain forever undiscovered.

Stuart could hear footsteps crossing the kitchen.

Was there anywhere he could hide? He looked around frantically, squinting in the darkness. Except that it wasn't darkness any longer. Another of the boards covering the front window was at that very moment being wrenched free and an arrow of light shot across the room, bouncing off the framed picture that he'd looked at earlier. And all of a sudden, he knew where he could go.

He scurried over to the fireplace, ducked down,

and crawled into it. It was larger than it looked. He could feel the draft stirring the air around him and he realized that if he stood at the back with his head and body actually up the chimney, then only his legs below the knee would be seen from the room, and since his jeans and sneakers were black, he'd be nearly invisible.

He got in as far as he could and then stood upright. With a painful thud, his head hit something hard.

"Start in the upstairs bathroom," said the voice coming along the passageway. "Get the tub out and then strip the piping. It's all copper."

Stuart ducked back down again, clutching his head. He could already feel a lump pushing up under his fingers. He half rose again, extended the other arm and felt around inside the chimney. He could feel the corners of a metal box. He gave it a shove, but it didn't move; one side of it seemed to be fixed to the brickwork. He stood up as much as he was able, his head crooked awkwardly to one side.

The clump of boots approached the fireplace.

"Any of the furnishings worth anything?" asked a second voice.

"A dealer came around and said he had a client for the big items. The rest is just trash."

The boots retreated again, and in a few moments Stuart heard the drumbeat of footsteps going up the stairs. In the living room all was momentarily quiet.

He took his chance. He crawled out from the fireplace and was about to make a dash for the back door, when the throbbing in his head seemed to push a thought into his brain.

A metal box.

A metal box fixed to the front of the chimney.

He stepped back to the fireplace and looked at the framed poster that hung above it.

The photograph of Great-Uncle Tony seemed to stare at him. Stuart gripped the bottom of the frame with one hand and lifted it up. There, behind the picture, was the closed door of a small safe inset into the chimney, firmly cemented into place. It had a little dial on the front, with the numbers one to twenty-nine printed around it. And beneath the dial were the words:

THE MINI HERCULES HOME SAFE
MANUFACTURED BY
HORTEN'S MIRACULOUS MECHANISMS

Stuart had seen safecracking done in films. He turned the wheel, first clockwise, then counterclockwise, then clockwise again. Nothing happened: no clicks, no clacks, no hidden springs. And he knew from films that nothing *would* happen unless he had exactly the right three-number combination.

He was just about to have another go when he heard footsteps coming back down the stairs, and he hastily lowered the picture and ran for the kitchen. The back door was still open so he galloped out and across the backyard, using the junk stepping stones that he'd first used only a week ago. As he vaulted from the old grill over the fence and into the neighbor's compost heap, someone shouted, "Hey, you!" but by that time Stuart knew he was safe.

It wasn't until he reached his bicycle that he realized that he'd left his great-uncle's back-door key sticking out of the lock.

And it wasn't until he arrived home and saw April Kingley looking out of the upstairs window of her house, the sun flashing off her glasses, and then saw her mouth drop open with shock, that he realized that he wasn't looking quite the same as when he'd left the house. The bathroom mirror confirmed it. He was completely coated with soot, and it took half an hour and most of his mother's Fruit 'n' Herb X-plozion shower gel, before he was acceptably clean again.

"That's a pleasant odor, if a trifle pungent," said his father, over a late breakfast. "Quince and tarragon?"

"Strawberry 'n' mint," said Stuart, between mouthfuls of cereal. "Dad, say you were a safecracker, and there was a safe with the numbers one to twenty-nine on the dial, and you didn't know the right combination. How long would it take you to try all of them?"

"Ah, a problem in probability," said his father. "Mathematical conundrums would be more your mother's area, I feel, but I seem to remember from my hours in the classroom that the number of combinations would be twenty-nine to the power of three."

"So that's twenty-nine times twenty-nine times twenty-nine," said Stuart. There was a pause while he fetched a calculator and tapped in the sum. "Twenty-four thousand, three hundred and eighty-nine possible combinations," he said, horrified.

Trying them all would be impossible, even if he actually managed to get back into the house again. No, his next task was obviously to find the correct three numbers.

Somehow.

His father crunched a piece of toast. "Do you have any plans for the matutinal hours?" he asked. "By which I mean, of, or related to, or occurring in the morning."

Stuart nodded. "Yes, I have. I'm going to . . ."

His voice tailed away as he looked at his dad. His father had such a nice face—never suspicious, never angry, never more than pleasantly puzzled—and Stuart was beginning to feel really bad about how many lies he'd told him over the last few days. On the other hand, if he said, *Yes, I have. I'm going to meet the blind sister of your missing uncle's fiancée in a bingo hall,* it wouldn't sound remotely believable.

"I'm going to go on another bike ride," he said.

CHAPTER 16

He reached the Gala Bingo Hall at ten to eleven. There was a sign on the sidewalk outside that read EARLY-BIRD SENIOR-CITIZEN SESSION 11 A.M. The doors were already open, and the foyer was heaving with old ladies. Stuart tried to edge in discreetly, but they all seemed very pleased to see him.

"Hello, young man. Here with Granny, are you?"

"Nice to see a young face. Eight, are you? Or seven, maybe?"

He looked around for Leonora, but all he could see was a wall of sensible coats. It occurred to him that he might as well try to do some research while he was waiting, so he smiled back at one of the women and asked if she remembered the Gala when it was a movie theater.

"Ooh, yes," she said. "Doing a school project, are you?"

"Mmm," said Stuart.

"Oh, it was lovely then," she continued. "A maitre d' at the door, all dressed in red and gold—he'd salute you when you went in—and a great big fish tank in the middle of the foyer." She turned to her friend. "Lorna, this young fellow wants to know if we remember this place when it was a movie theater."

"Remember it?" said Lorna, who was all dressed in blue, including her shoes and glasses. "We practically used to live here, didn't we, Vi?"

"Lived here," confirmed Vi. "Saw every film they ever showed. We used to sit in the balcony, and I always had a strawberry cone and you always had a bag of toffees."

"Oh, those toffees," said Lorna, "I'd forgotten about those. There was a machine just by the ticket office, wasn't there? You put in threepence and you got a little bag full. Always exactly the same number of toffees."

"Baker's dozen," said Vi.

"Unluckily for my teeth!" added Lorna. Both women laughed.

"Is it still here somewhere—the toffee machine?" asked Stuart.

"Ooh no, love, everything went when it was turned into a bingo hall. I remember them tearing it all out—this place was just an empty shell."

A bell started to ring, and in the sudden shift of bodies Stuart spotted a guide dog and squeezed through to where Leonora stood waiting.

"It's me," he said, putting a hand on her arm. "Stuart."

She smiled, and the dog sniffed Stuart's knees suspiciously. On the other side of the foyer, a man in a smart suit flung open the doors into the main hall.

"Have you ever played bingo?" asked Leonora as the sensible coats surged into the hall.

"No," said Stuart.

The next thirty minutes was a hideous embarrassment. Surrounded by people about seventy years older than himself and sitting next to someone who was actually blind, Stuart thought he might have a chance of winning. He was wrong. The caller announced the numbers at the speed of light, everyone else had a row of at least six bingo cards while Stuart only had one, and he still couldn't keep up. At one point he was so flustered that he dropped his pen on the floor, and one of the old ladies actually patted him on the head as he scrambled around for it.

When Leonora, who had special Braille cards, won a voucher for a shampoo and perm at a local hairdresser, the caller shouted out, "Let the little lad collect it! Let's have a big hand for the little feller!" And everyone applauded as he clumped to the front, beet red.

"That was very, very kind of you," said Leonora when he got back to his seat. "Now, let's go to the café upstairs here and have a chat."

She bought him a slice of banana cream pie and they sat at a table by the window. The dog rested its chin on Stuart's knee while he ate.

"Is the pie nice?" asked Leonora.

"Fantastic!" said Stuart.

Leonora laughed. "You sound just like your

great-uncle. That was his favorite word when he was a boy."

"When he was a *boy*? You mean you knew him when he was my age?"

"I grew up in the house that I live in now. At the bottom of our yard, on the other side of the wall, was the Horten factory. When they weren't at school, Tony and his brother Ray—your grandfather— were there all the time, playing in the yard, learning the trade. Well, Ray was learning the trade. Tony was practicing magic most of the time. I wonder whether you look like him. I remember that he had the most marvelous green eyes."

Stuart looked at her own eyes, blue but sightless. "But—" he began.

"I could see then," she said. "Never very well, but enough to watch and remember. It wasn't until I was much older, after I'd left college and started teaching, that I went completely blind." She leaned forward and ruffled the dog's ears. "And luckily for me, I've got Pluto now," she said.

"I haven't got green eyes," said Stuart. "But I'm very short, just like Tony."

"Oh, *short*," she said dismissively, waving a hand. "Tony's height didn't matter. He was short in the way that a stick of dynamite is short. Crackling with energy and ideas. And I can show you exactly what he looked like as a youngster."

She fished in her bag and brought out a scrapbook. "This was made by my big sister Lily," she said, and her voice trembled a little. She took a breath. "It was her engagement present for Tony. Have a look at the first page."

Stuart took the book from her and turned it the right way up. The words *Our Story* were inscribed in curly writing on the front. He opened it to the first page, and his stomach jolted. There was a faded photograph of a small boy, grinning from beneath the brim of a top hat. It was the very same small boy that he'd seen pulling faces on every single page of the book in the library.

"Is that my great-uncle?" he asked. "The boy in the top hat?"

"That's him," Leonora nodded. "That photograph was taken on the day he earned his first wages for magic. He performed at a children's party and was paid two shillings and sixpence, all in threepences. He was so proud. He called it his magical money and said that he'd never, ever spend it."

Stuart stared at the picture. Great-Uncle Tony was gripping a wand with one hand, but his other hand was held out toward the camera. In the palm was a cluster of coins.

"Stuart, how did you find me?" asked Leonora abruptly.

"I put a threepence in an old Horten's weighing machine," said Stuart. "I know it sounds a bit mad, but that's what I did. And the needle swung around to seventy-nine, and the words GRAVE STREET FLAT E were scratched into the paintwork next to it."

He waited to see if Leonora would laugh or scoff, but she said nothing.

"And before that," said Stuart, feeling reckless, "I put a threepence into a phone booth and it rang even though the line had been cut."

Again, Leonora was silent.

"And I found those threepences in a trick money box just like the one you showed me, and yesterday

I found an old note in the false bottom of the tin, and it's from Great-Uncle Tony. He meant it for my father. He wanted him to find the workshop."

This time Leonora made a little squeaking noise and her cheeks flushed rose-pink. "I knew it!" she said. "I knew Tony was behind it. Did the note say anything else?"

"It said that he had to go away and that he might not be able to get back."

Leonora nodded.

"Do you know where he went?" asked Stuart.

"No," answered Leonora. "But I know *why* he went. He went to find my sister Lily."

"Why? Where did she go?"

Leonora placed her hand on Pluto's head, as if to steady herself. "Some people thought that she died in the factory fire in nineteen forty," she said. "Some people thought she must have left Tony after an argument. You're probably the first person I've ever met who'll believe the truth."

CHAPTER 17

"When the war started," said Leonora, "the Horten factory stopped making its usual items and started making swivel joints for anti-aircraft guns. It was important war work, which meant that your grandfather, Ray, wasn't called up for the army. He was allowed to stay and look after the factory."

"And Great-Uncle Tony?" asked Stuart.

"He was below the minimum height requirement."

"Too short to be a soldier?"

"Yes. So he stayed in Beeton too and became an air-raid warden, and he got on with what he liked doing best, which was inventing new stage tricks. He was really beginning to make a name for himself."

"Teeny-Tiny Tony Horten," said Stuart.

"That's right. People still went to the theater during the war. They were desperate for entertainment, and he had more bookings than ever. And then Ray was asked to travel around to other factories to advise on making swivel joints, and Tony said not to worry and that he'd look after everything while his brother was away."

"Oh," said Stuart, sensing doom.

"One evening, Tony and Lily were in the workshop. Night shift had just started in the factory. Tony was rehearsing a new illusion for his next tour. He never bothered with the things that other magicians used, like silly silk handkerchiefs or doves or playing cards. He might not have been interested in the family factory, but he was a brilliant engineer in the tradition of Victorian stage magicians—and there had been one of those in the family, once. Did you know that?"

"The Great Hortini," supplied Stuart, dimly remembering the librarian droning on about the history of the Hortens.

"That's right. Well, Tony was inspired by that,

and what he built for his shows were beautiful mechanisms: magical doors into nowhere, pyramids with sliding walls, mirrored arches with a hundred reflections. I remember going to a performance and, though I couldn't see the stage clearly, I could see the glitter and brilliance of it, and I could see Lily disappearing and reappearing in her silver costume, and I could hear the gasps from the audience."

Leonora stopped speaking for a while and Stuart waited, picking up crumbs from his banana cream pie with a damp finger, idly watching a white dove that had landed on the window ledge just outside.

"I'm sorry," said Leonora, after another minute. "I started thinking about Lily and Tony. They were both hot-tempered people, forever arguing—two firecrackers in a box—but they loved each other so much. Being with them was like warming your hands on a bonfire. I've had a busy life, but there hasn't been a single day when I haven't missed them. And as I get older, I seem to miss them more and more."

The dove on the window ledge clattered its wings and took off again, swooping toward the sidewalk opposite the bingo hall and almost landing on the foot of a man in green trousers, who was standing in the shadow of a shop front.

"So, that evening at the factory," continued Leonora, "Tony had been working on the Well of Wishes. It was a very elaborate piece of machinery, with a secret compartment for Lily to hide in. The idea was that at the very beginning of the show Tony would drop a coin into the well and wish for a beautiful assistant, and then she'd appear. And at the end, as a little joke, *she'd* drop in the coin and wish for them both to disappear and off they'd go.

"So he was trying to perfect this, doing the trick over and over again, and Lily was tired—she was working as a nurse at the local hospital during the day, and she wanted to go home. They had one of their arguments, there was a great deal of shouting, and during the course of it the coin that Tony had been using to drop into the well was hurled across the room by Lily, landing somewhere unreachable. And Tony, trying to patch up the argument, said he'd give her a very, *very* special coin for the trick, and he went to the factory safe and took out the purse of money that he'd earned from that first-ever magic show. It was two shillings and sixpence, all in threepences—ten coins in all."

"His magical money," said Stuart, barely breathing.

"He gave Lily the purse, and at that moment the siren sounded. There had already been a couple of false alarms that day, but Tony was an air-raid warden and he took his duties seriously. He went into the main factory to make sure that all the workers entered the shelter, and then he returned to the workshop.

"Lily wasn't there. Her coat was still on the peg, and her shoes and handbag were beside it on the floor, so he knew she hadn't left. He called and searched. The air-raid warning was real this time; he could hear the bomber engines overhead and the clatter of incendiary bombs dropping outside the factory. Tony kept searching. He looked in all the secret compartments of all the stage illusions. He shouted Lily's name. And then he smelled smoke. An incendiary had landed in the gutter on the roof. He climbed up through a skylight to try to dislodge it, but a fire was already taking hold. He hurried back to the workshop and searched again, desperately, frantically. Smoke was beginning to fill the factory, and he could hear the fire engines approaching, bells ringing.

"And then he saw something on the floor. It was the purse. He picked it up, and something made him count the threepences inside. There were only nine left.

"The smoke was so thick by now that Tony could hardly see. He started to grope his way across the workshop toward the Well of Wishes, and then he must have lost consciousness, because the next thing he remembered was waking up outside the factory.

"He'd been rescued by a fireman, and Horten's Miraculous Mechanisms was ablaze. Every stick of it burned. No trace of Lily was ever found. Plenty of the workers had heard them arguing, and some people assumed that she'd taken the chance to leave. It was easy to disappear during the war—people moved around all the time and you could start again somewhere else, without anyone knowing. But Tony knew that she hadn't left the factory. He was half mad with guilt and fear. You see"—she paused and moved her lips silently a couple of times, as if trying to work out what to say next—"you see, although he was a magician, he had never actually believed in *magic*. Everything he'd done had been a mixture of engineering and entertainment, and now a purse full of coins had changed all that he knew, all that he understood. He told me that he was certain that Lily was alive somewhere, and he thought that if he could rebuild the Well of Wishes—if he could recreate it *exactly*—then he could follow her.

"So he started working secretly. He locked himself away; he gave performances only in order to raise the money to carry on with his search. His only wish in life was to find Lily. And one day, four years after the fire, in the hidden workshop, I think he succeeded."

"You mean that's when he disappeared?" asked Stuart.

Leonora nodded.

"But where did Lily go?" he asked. "What did she wish for? Where did the coin take her?"

"I don't know," said Leonora. "I've spent fifty years wondering."

"But if I track down the workshop," said Stuart, "then maybe we'll find out."

She smiled, her face looking suddenly very young. "Yes, maybe," she said, and she held out the scrapbook toward him. "Take this. I'd like you to have it. I don't need it any more, all the pictures are in my memory now."

CHAPTER 18

Cycling with a scrapbook under his arm wasn't easy, and halfway home, as Stuart rounded a corner, the book slid out from under his elbow, spinning ahead of him along the road, pages fluttering. A newspaper clipping detached itself from the last page, and Stuart got off his bike and chased the slip of paper along the sidewalk.

As he grabbed it and shoved it back into the book, he realized that he could hear running footsteps behind him and he turned and saw a chunky man in green trousers tearing around the corner at full speed, arms pumping like a sprinter. A second later the man saw Stuart, stopped dead, spun on his heel, and darted back out of view again.

Stuart stood staring. He'd recognized the man. It was Clifford, the trainee magician. Overhead, a white dove flew in a lazy loop and settled on top of a lamppost.

Jeannie's ordered him to follow me, thought Stuart. *She's hoping that I'll lead the way to the workshop.*

He got back on his bike again and pedaled off very slowly. He took the next left, cycled halfway along the road, then shoved his bike under a parked car and crouched behind it. Sure enough, thirty seconds later, pounding footsteps approached. They thundered straight past and around the next corner. Grinning, Stuart got his bike out again and rode home in the other direction.

He felt full of purpose and energy, and as soon as he'd hidden the scrapbook in his room and had eaten a bag of potato chips, a ham sandwich, four pickled onions, a lump of cheese, two more pickled onions, and another bag of potato chips, he was ready to set out again.

"Whither your current destination?" asked his father.

"The library. Mom said they'd phoned me yesterday about a book."

"Oh, splendid. Do you mind if I accompany you?"

They walked there together, and Stuart waited until his father was transfixed by volume three of *The History of European Lexicography* before he set off for the information desk.

"Aha!" said the same man as before, his glasses still dangling on a chain around his neck. "It's our local history scholar. Stay there just a moment."

He disappeared into a back room, and Stuart waited impatiently, drumming his fingers on the desktop.

"And here we are," said the man, reappearing. "We've re-inserted the missing photograph. Do not forget the gloves."

Stuart took the little book over to a table and eased the white gloves onto his fingers. He opened *Modern Beeton: A Photographic Record* and spotted a little paragraph that he hadn't noticed before, tucked away in tiny print at the bottom of the title page:

This booklet was commissioned by Horten's Miraculous Mechanisms as a permanent record of the firm's contribution to the life of twentieth-century Beeton.

Stuart started to thumb through, and this time it was like looking at a family album. The little boy that was Great-Uncle Tony gazed out from every page, making a different face in each. First in the phone booth, then beside the weighing machine, then by the swimming-pool turnstile . . .

"And *that's* the order I found them in!" said Stuart out loud.

There was a fierce "*Shhh!*" from the man behind the counter.

Stuart hunched down, embarrassed, took a piece of scrap paper and a pencil, and started to make a list:

1. Main Street. Phone booth. FOUND IT.
2. Station. Weighing machine. FOUND IT.

3. Outdoor swimming pool. Turnstile.
   FOUND IT.
4. Movie theater/bingo hall. Toffee machine.
5. Gas station.

In this photo, Great-Uncle Tony was doing a handstand against the side of the building, where Stuart had seen the bicycle-repair sign. His booted feet were resting on a tall metal box on four legs.

Stuart stared at the box for a while, then shrugged and wrote "???? machine" before turning the page.

6. Fairground.

Pictured were a Ferris wheel and a merry-go-round, a shoot-the-duck stall, and a cotton-candy booth. There was even a ghost train, decorated with some badly drawn phantoms and a wildly screaming girl. Great-Uncle Tony was in the photograph, of course, in the background, standing on one foot and miming a kick at a passing boy with the other. Just behind him was an odd-looking object. It looked like a huge, upright ruler as tall as Stuart's father. At the top of it was a round bell, and written down the side of the ruler were the words:

TEST
YOUR
STRENGTH

What appeared to be an enormous mallet on a rope was hanging from a hook beside it.

Stuart added the words *Strength machine?* to the list. Then he turned the page and saw, for the first time, the missing photo.

Ancient and modern together: a young man of today encounters the past read the caption. The "young man" was Great-Uncle Tony, and for once he was right at the center of the picture. He was standing in a large, rather grand room, gazing at a glass cabinet filled with what looked like tiny buttons. Behind him were other cabinets, also filled with buttons. Stuart frowned, wrote:

7. ????

And then he turned to the last picture.

8. Bandstand.

The bandstand stood in the middle of the park. The bulletin board fixed to its base had a poster that said SUNDAY CONCERTS, and next to it, on the grass, sat Uncle Tony playing an imaginary trumpet. Stuart looked at the photo close-up, his nose almost touching the page, and then again from a distance. He even turned it upside down, just in case he was missing something. Finally he gave up and turned back to the photograph of Uncle Tony and the buttons.

Cabinets of buttons. Shiny buttons. Shiny metal buttons.

No, Stuart realized suddenly. They weren't *buttons* at all.

Hurriedly he returned the book to the desk. You weren't supposed to run in the library, but he ran, and found his father in the reference section.

"Dad," he said breathlessly. "Remember a few days ago you said something about coins to me?"

"Coins . . .?" said his father dreamily, his finger still marking his place in *The History of European Lexicography*, his brain elsewhere.

"*Coins*," repeated Stuart, slowly and firmly. "You said something about a collection being of interest to a newsymatolly something."

"Aha!" His father's face lit up. "You're talking about the Horten Numismatology Collection in Beeton Museum. Apparently it's splendid."

"The *Horten* Numi-whatsit Collection?"

"Yes."

"What, it's named after our *family*?"

"I believe so."

"But you didn't tell me it was called that!"

"Oh, didn't I?" said his father, with infuriating vagueness.

"*No*. Never mind. Can we go there?" asked Stuart. "Can we go there *right now*?"

BEETON MUSEUM

CHAPTER 19

"Hello," said the woman at the desk. "Does this little fellow want the young explorer's backpack?"

"No," said Stuart.

"It's got stickers!" said the woman, encouragingly.

"No," said Stuart more firmly.

His father was standing beside him in the foyer of the museum gazing at a scale model of a Roman catapult.

"Of course, the Latin name, *ballista*, is the root of our modern word *ballistics*," he said, to no one in particular.

Stuart was looking at the museum map on the wall. Most of the rooms seemed to be filled with an exhibition about Beeton during the Second World War, but there were one or two that were labeled MISCELLANEOUS COLLECTIONS. He needed a bit of time to poke about on his own.

"If you're interested in ballistae," said a loud voice behind him, "then you'll find a further collection of Roman siege engines in room four."

Stuart turned to see a man in a checked suit. He was wearing a badge that said ROD FELTON, CHIEF CURATOR, and he looked enormously enthusiastic, in a toothy sort of way.

"In particular, there is the post-classical example known as an onager," he added.

Stuart's father looked up keenly. "I believe the name *onager* is also the Latin for *wild ass*," he said.

Rod Felton almost jumped with delight. "That's absolutely correct. It's derived from the kicking action of the machine, which in turn is the result of torsional pressure from a twisted rope. And the later medieval version, the mangonel, was also a . . ."

With any luck, thought Stuart, they'll be yakking for half an hour. Unnoticed, he slipped past the desk into the museum.

Hardly anyone else was in there. He passed a 1940s classroom and a 1940s grocery store, and then walked through a screened-off section containing a backyard air-raid shelter with a set of bunk beds inside. As he did so, a siren sounded and all the lights went off, and there was a short pause before a tape of bombing noises began. He carried on walking.

"Beeton in Wartime" continued—there were photographs and leaflets and posters, and a large-scale model of the town showing where bombs had dropped and where underground shelters had been built. Stuart lingered briefly over the model. It was very neatly made, with lots of detail, and he was just tracing the route he'd taken the day before when he heard the curator's voice bellowing from somewhere behind him.

"The weapon known as the trebuchet, or trebucket, on the other hand, was employed in the Middle Ages during sieges in order to . . ."

Stuart broke into a jog and raced through the rest of the wartime exhibition. The next room contained Roman weaponry and armor, and the one after that a collection of Victorian tools and farm implements, as well as a large fake cow being milked by a huge fake milkmaid and an enormous fake horse being shoed by a giant fake blacksmith.

Stuart hurried toward the next door, and paused. There was a small brass plaque screwed to the central panel:

THE NUMISMATOLOGICAL ROOM
ENDOWED 1922 BY
HORTEN'S MIRACULOUS MECHANISMS

He pushed open the door and found himself staring at the view he'd seen earlier in the photograph: the glass cabinet containing Roman coins, the array of coin-filled cases beyond. Behind them was a tall row of display boards, showing HOW MONEY IS MADE, with cartoonish illustrations.

Stuart walked around the display and caught his breath. Beneath the window stood three large, old, coin-operated machines.

He walked toward them, feeling as if he were moving in slow motion. They were situated on stone blocks, roped off from the rest of the room, and a sign on the wall above them read:

Vintage coin-operated machinery from a variety of Beeton businesses, manufactured by Horten's Miraculous Mechanisms. Collected and donated to Beeton Museum by Mr. Anthony Horten. DO NOT TOUCH!

Stuart read the sign again, scarcely able to believe his eyes. *Collected and donated by Mr. Anthony Horten!* It was as if Great-Uncle Tony were standing right here, grinning, giving him the thumbs up, and urging him onward.

Three machines, thought Stuart.

Three numbers needed for the safe.

And all at once he knew, with utter certainty, that this was where he would find the combination.

He ducked under the rope and climbed onto the stone blocks.

To his left stood the movie theater toffee machine. It was a square metal box on legs, with the words CHOOSE OUR CHEWS! stamped on the front, and a picture of a toffee with a bite taken out of it. There was a slot for a coin at the top and a hole for dispensing the toffees at the bottom.

The machine on the right was identical in appearance apart from the wording, which read:

BICYCLE TIRE REPAIR KITS

In the center stood the machine from the fairground. It was much more eye-catching than the other two: the lettering was in yellow and red, the bell at the top had been brightly polished, and the giant mallet was glossy with black paint. At the base of the machine stood something that looked like an iron mushroom, a little more than a foot and a half high, and behind it there was a diagram of a stick man hitting the mushroom with the mallet. ARE YOU A WEAKLING OR A MUSCLE MAN? ONLY THE TRULY STRONG CAN RING THE BELL! was printed next to the diagram.

Stuart looked around to check that no one had come into the room, and then he stepped forward, already feeling for a threepence in his pocket.

According to the order of photos in the book from the library, the movie theater toffee machine should come first.

He pushed the coin into the slot and pulled the lever. There was a brief rattling sound and then the slither of something coming down a chute, and a loud thud as it reached the bottom. He reached in and removed a small paper bag. Inside it was a solid, slightly sticky clump of toffees, immovably welded together by heat and time. Hurriedly, Stuart had another feel around inside the hole, but there was nothing else there.

Shoving the bag into his pocket, he took out another threepence and moved quickly across to the machine on the right, the one that dispensed bicycle tire repair kits.

And then he paused, reaching out a disbelieving hand. The slot for the coins had been covered with a thin strip of metal. It was held tightly in place by two large screws. Desperately, uselessly, he pried at them with his fingernails. He could have yelled in frustration.

Suddenly, he remembered the tools in the Victorian room. He ducked under the rope again and raced back there.

It was empty of visitors. The tools were fixed to the wall in fan-shaped arrangements. He could see a display of hammers and one of chisels, and finally, with a leap of the heart, he spotted an entire array of screwdrivers of different sizes, with age-darkened blades and smooth wooden handles.

They were just out of his reach.

He stood on tiptoe, but they were still too high for him so he looked around for something to stand on and saw that the large fake milkmaid was seated on a three-legged stool.

She was fixed in a sitting position, so he lifted her up (she was surprisingly heavy) and propped her headfirst against a wagon wheel. Then he grabbed the stool and climbed onto it. He could now reach the screwdrivers. Each was fastened to the wall with a pair of plastic loops. He pulled at the handle of one of the largest. The loops snapped easily—far more easily than he'd expected—and he found himself wavering backward, stepping into midair, sticking out a hand to break his fall.

And what broke his fall was the milkmaid's backside. She lurched forward, shoving the wagon wheel with her head, and at that exact moment the curator and Stuart's father entered the room.

Stuart, lying on his back, clutching the screwdriver, could see exactly what was going to happen, and he could do nothing, *nothing* to stop it.

The wheel trundled across the room and hit the cow, the cow leaned on the blacksmith, the blacksmith toppled onto the horse, and the horse keeled over sideways, hitting the floor with the most enormous crash. There was another smaller crash as one of its back legs dropped off, and then a final, tiny clatter as it lost an ear.

The silence seemed to go on and on.

"Hello, Dad," said Stuart.

CHAPTER 20

Stuart and his father didn't talk much on the way home.

Stuart hadn't been able to think of a believable explanation for the horse-smashing incident, so he had simply said, "I'm really, really sorry," to the curator and, "It was an accident," both of which statements were true.

His father had silently written out a check.

The curator had stood in the front entrance and watched them leave. He hadn't actually said, "Go away, you disgusting vandal and never darken these doors again," but he might as well have done so.

Halfway home, it started to rain heavily.

"I really am really, really sorry, Dad," said Stuart, dripping, as they turned the corner onto Beech Road.

"I know you are," said his father. But he looked worried, as well as soaked. When they got into the house, Stuart saw him pick up the phone right away.

Stuart went to his room and flopped on the bed. He felt exhausted. He had wrecked the museum and humiliated his father, and all he had to show for it was a bag of inedible toffee.

He took it out of his pocket and looked at it.

He'd been certain that each of the museum machines would provide him with a number, but what number could he extract from an unmarked paper bag containing a large brown lump—one huge toffee where there had once been a handful?

And then, all of a sudden, he seemed to hear a chirpy voice: *You put in threepence and you got a little bag full. Always exactly the same number of toffees.* Lorna, the woman in the blue glasses at the bingo hall, had told him that. And then her friend, Vi, had chipped in with the precise number. A dozen. She'd said a dozen!

So if the first number was twelve, and he had to guess at the other two, how many goes at the safe would it take before he got the combination right? He fetched his calculator, tapped out 29 × 29, and groaned. That was still *far* too many. And in less than a week's time, Uncle Tony's house would be demolished, and the safe lost forever, crushed under tons of rubble.

He had to sneak back into the museum. Secretly.

He had to sneak back, undo a couple of screws on one machine, and then swing an enormous great hammer in order to ring a very large bell on the other. Secretly.

And if he didn't manage it he would never find the workshop, and more than that, he would never find out what had happened to Great-Uncle Tony or to Lily.

It was then that he remembered the scrapbook Leonora had given him. He reached down and pulled it out from under his bed, brushing dust balls from the cover.

He looked again at the first photograph, of Great-Uncle Tony holding the threepences, and then he began to turn the pages. The first few pictures were all of children: of Lily, presumably, and her little sister Leonora, of Tony and his big brother Ray—Lily and Tony always grinning, fighting, shouting, jumping, a blur of energy and action, Leonora always holding a book, looking shyly at the camera from behind thick spectacles, Ray always serious and slightly disapproving.

Photograph followed photograph; gradually the children grew up. The boys acquired mustaches, Lily smoked a daring cigarette, Leonora held up a certificate from Saint Cuthbert's Training College, showing that she'd qualified as a teacher. There were flyers from Tony's magic shows and ecstatic reviews of his performances, and pictures of Lily in glamorous costumes, and on the final page of the book, crumpled and slightly torn, was the yellowed newspaper clipping that had fallen onto the road the day before.

Stuart smoothed it out. It was the top half of a page from the *Beeton Advertiser* of September 1940.

It showed a photograph of Great-Uncle Tony and Lily, holding hands and grinning hugely at the camera. He was wearing a tin helmet with a w on the front, and she was in nurse's uniform.

BEETON CELEBRITY TO MARRY

"Teeny-Tiny" Tony Horten and his lovely assistant Lily Vickers pose together after announcing their engagement. Speaking to our reporter yesterday, Mr. Horten (who is also a volunteer air-raid warden for the Beeton Park area) said—

Stuart heard a soft noise, like a sharp click. And then another. And another. Stuart hauled himself up and went over to the window. April Kingley was standing on the sidewalk holding a handful of pebbles.

"*Go away*," he mouthed through the glass.

She shook her head and threw another one.

Stuart opened the window. "What do you want?" he asked as rudely as possible.

"Did you know you're being watched?" asked April.

"Yes," he said. "By you."

She shook her head. "Seriously. There's a man about forty years old, a bit fat, dressed in green trousers, with no distinguishing features apart from a white dove that keeps flapping around wherever he's hiding. Which is currently behind the hedge at number twenty-two. He turned up not long after you got home covered in mud again. And then when you went off with your dad a bit later, he was sneaking along about fifty feet behind. Incidentally, why *were* you covered in mud for the second day in a row?"

"It wasn't mud. It was soot."

"All right, why were you covered in soot?"

"It's none of your business," said Stuart, annoyed to learn that Clifford was still following him. He closed the window.

A few more pebbles smacked against the glass. He opened the window again. "Stop it," he said.

April folded her arms and looked at him with her head tilted to one side. Her expression was incredibly irritating, a mixture of condescension and sympathy. "I think you're in some kind of trouble," she said.

"No, I'm not."

"And I really think you should tell someone about it. Me, preferably, because I'm really good at keeping secrets, and because I'm quite brave, and also because my journalistic contacts—"

"You don't have any journalistic contacts," Stuart said. "*You're ten years old.*"

"My journalistic contacts," she continued determinedly, "mean that I'm a really useful person to know."

"Go away," said Stuart.

"And I'm a fast runner," she added. "And I always win at dares, and my report card said that I never take no for an answer."

Stuart started to close the window.

"And I'm *bored*!" April shouted. "I'm really, really, really *bored*. I can't find any crime to report, and my sisters aren't interested in investigative journalism. All they want to do is copy stuff out of the paper. Anyway," she added, "I bet you need help."

He hesitated, his hand on the window latch.

He did need help. Without it he'd never get back into the museum, and he'd never find the safe combination, and he couldn't give up now, he just couldn't.

He took a deep breath. "Okay," he said. "I'll meet you in the yard in two minutes."

When he got outside, Stuart wished he'd chosen somewhere else to meet. He'd forgotten that April was tall enough to rest her chin on the top of the fence, whereas he could only see over into the yard next door if he stood on tiptoe.

"So," said April, looking down at him, "what's going on?"

Stuart thought hard. He didn't really trust her, so it would be best, he decided, to give her as little information as possible, and not to mention the coins or the machines, or even Great-Uncle Tony. He would have to be very, very clever about it.

"All right," he said. "If you needed to spend twenty minutes in one of the rooms in Beeton

Museum without being disturbed by anyone, how would you do it?"

"What's this, a quiz?" asked April, frowning.

"In a way," he replied mysteriously.

"Well, what do you need to do for those twenty minutes?" she asked. "Do you want to borrow something?"

"No."

"Steal something?"

"*No.*"

"Have a go on one of those old-fashioned slot machines in the back room?"

His jaw dropped. "How do you know?"

"Everyone wants a go on those. They lock them up when school trips come around. They'll only work with old threepenny bits. Have you got some?"

"Er . . ."

"I bet you have. Where did you find them?"

"Er . . ."

"Did they belong to your great-uncle Tony who had the house? Did they?"

Stuart nodded dumbly. It was hopeless. She was just too clever for him.

"You might as well tell me everything," said April. "Go on. Please. *Please*."

In a way, it was a relief to be able to tell someone the whole story. April listened carefully, her expression serious, the sunlight bouncing off her spectacles. When he'd finished speaking, she was silent for a very long time, and then she cleared her throat.

"I don't believe in magic," she said.

"Nor me," said Stuart. "But then neither did Great-Uncle Tony until the night of the fire."

She nodded slowly. "And as a crime reporter," she said, "I've developed an uncanny ability to spot when someone is telling the truth. And I know you're telling the truth." She closed her eyes for about three seconds and then opened them again. "Right," she said. "I've got a plan."

"What, already?"

"Yup." She grinned. "Told you I was good."

"I haven't heard the plan yet," said Stuart coldly.

"It's quite simple," she declared, "and we can do it tomorrow. Tomorrow night. Now, listen . . ."

CHAPTER 21

The next morning Stuart woke quite late. He lay in bed for a while, idly listening to a pigeon cooing outside his window, and then a sudden thought struck him. He scrambled out of bed, and pulled open the curtain. What he saw wasn't a pigeon, but a white dove—Clifford's white dove—and it fluttered up from the windowsill and flew in a wide circle above the road, settling at last on the top of a hedge. A hand appeared above the hedge and made a grab for the bird. The dove flew off, leaving a single white tail feather behind.

Stuart closed the curtain again. He could hear another unusual noise, he realized. It was the sound of his mother's voice, coming from downstairs. Which meant that she was still at home halfway through the morning, on a *weekday*.

"Hi, Mom," he said, coming into the kitchen a few minutes later. "Are you ill?"

"No, no." She smiled breezily. "Just fancied a day off. I wanted a little bit of rest, after the move—organizing all our clothes and shoes and so on, and putting stuff in the attic."

"Okay," he said, not terribly interested.

"Are you doing anything today?" she asked.

"No," he said. Then he remembered the plan. "I mean, yes. Yes I am. You know those girls who came around the other night?"

She nodded.

"They invited me over to their house this evening. It's next door."

"Oh, that's *lovely*!" said his mother, looking so thrilled you'd think she'd won a million dollars. "What are you going to do there?"

"One of them's making a pizza," said Stuart. "And then we're going to watch a movie on TV. I'll be out quite late. Till at least ten o'clock. Is that okay?"

"Of course it is. It's the summer," said his mother. "What's the film?"

"It's about volcanoes."

"Shield, cinder cone, or composite?"

"Don't know," said Stuart.

"Is it cinema vérité, or is there a fictional component?" asked his father.

"Don't know that either," said Stuart. "Anyway, they've asked me to come around there at about five."

Next door, he knew, April would be telling *her* parents that she'd been invited to Stuart's for the evening. The plan was simple and cunning. *It might,* he thought, *actually work.*

The day seemed to pass slowly. Stuart spent most of it lying in front of the television, but every now and again he got up and checked out of the front window. He didn't actually see Clifford, but a couple of times he spotted the dove, still circling the rooftops.

Upstairs, his father worked in the study and his mother opened and shut closets and moved things around. Once she popped her head into the living room and asked him if he'd seen his walking boots since moving to Beeton. He hadn't.

At last it was ten to five. Stuart stood in the hall and shouted a casual, "Bye, see you later!" up the stairs. He opened the front door, counted to three, and then shut it again, deliberately noisily, before tiptoeing back through the house and into the yard.

April was waiting on her side of the fence. "There you are," she said. "Clifford's definitely still out front, so we'll have to escape the back way. Take this; you'll need it."

She passed a kitchen stool over the fence to him, and after a moment of irritation, Stuart stood on it and climbed over to her side. There was a piece of rope tied to one leg of the stool, and she hauled it across after him.

"Where are your sisters?" asked Stuart, glancing at the back windows of her house.

"Printing off the next edition of the *Beech Road Guardian*," she said. "Hurry up, can't you?" She had already placed the stool beside the next fence, and they both climbed over, picking their way through a cluster of plastic gnomes and around a miniature wishing well.

"Only three more backyards to go," said April.

The final fence bordered a small paved alleyway. April tucked the stool behind a garbage can and then tiptoed along to the corner and peered around.

"He's still there!" she hissed. "He really is the most useless spy. Anyone with half a brain could outwit him."

"Come *on*!" said Stuart. "The museum closes at six."

They ran side by side out of the other end of the alley, and then slowed to a fast walk for the rest of the half-mile to the museum.

"Right," said April, stopping dead when they were within sight of the main door. "Repeat the plan to me again."

"I don't need to," said Stuart. "I know it."

"But we should go through it again, step by step."

"Why?"

"Because that's what makes a good plan into a great plan."

"Okay," said Stuart. "We go in, you start a conversation with the ticket woman so that I can sneak past, I go to the bathroom to open the window, we hide somewhere, we come out when the museum's closed and everyone's gone home, we put the coins in the machines, we get out through the open window. Now can we *go*?"

"Did you bring a flashlight?"

"Yes."

"Did you bring a screwdriver?"

"Yes."

"Did you bring the threepenny bits in a proper wallet, rather than just letting them jingle around in your pocket?"

"*YES*."

"There's no need to get cross," she said brightly, setting off again. Stuart took a deep breath and followed her.

The first problem was that standing right in the middle of the foyer was the museum curator, Rod Felton. Stuart ducked behind a large shrub outside the entrance and beckoned to April.

"That's the one who saw me wreck the horse,"

he whispered. "Go and talk to him about Roman ballistics."

"About what?"

"Weapons that throw things," said Stuart, feeling a bit like his father. "And ask about siege engines."

"What are those?"

"Things for knocking over walls."

April nodded and scurried into the museum. Peering from the undergrowth, Stuart could see the electrifying effect of the word *ballistics* on the curator. A conversation began, Rod Felton waving his arms around and April nodding keenly. She was good at this sort of thing, Stuart had to admit. If only she wasn't so patronizing and annoying and incredibly, unbearably bossy.

The curator guided April to the model of the Roman ballista and she started pointing at different parts of it and asking questions, lots of questions. And the woman at the ticket desk was writing down something while talking on the phone.

Stuart seized his chance. He bent over and ran at a crouch straight through the open doors, past the back of Rod Felton, and into the first room of the museum. Then he straightened up and, pretending to be a normal visitor, followed the signs to the men's bathroom.

There he found the second problem. He'd intended to unlatch a window so that April and he could get out of the museum later on, but the only window was quite high up and he couldn't reach it. Beeton Museum seemed to be full of things that he couldn't reach.

Stuart exited the bathrom, heard the words ". . . could hurl a half-ton boulder more than one hundred yards with the use of twisted sheepskin thongs . . ." coming around the corner, and dove back in again.

Immediately, there was a crackling noise and a click. "*Beeton Museum will be closing in five minutes,*" said a voice from a loudspeaker above his head. "*Please make your way to the exit.*"

Stuart peered out of the bathroom again. Visitors trickled past, heading homeward. There was, he noticed, a door marked JANITOR just opposite. He was about to investigate when April sprinted around the corner, spotted him, and gestured frantically for him to follow. They ran past the wartime classroom and the wartime grocery store.

"*Here!*" hissed April, swerving at the sign that read AIR-RAID SHELTER and hurrying down two steps into the dark interior. It was a very small shelter, just a curl of corrugated iron, containing a bunk bed and a bench.

"*In there,*" whispered April, pointing toward the lower bed. She climbed the ladder to the top bunk, while at the bottom Stuart pulled the blanket over himself and lay as flat as possible. The blanket smelled of wet dog. The mattress was lumpy and slightly damp.

"*Beeton Museum will be closing in one minute,*" said the voice on the loudspeaker.

Stuart counted very slowly to a thousand, trying to breathe through his mouth so as not to have to smell the blanket.

All was quiet outside the shelter. He was just about to speak when he heard a distant whining noise that grew gradually louder. It was, he realized, an electric floor polisher. Slowly, the noise passed them and faded away.

Stuart started counting again. When he got to eight thousand, two hundred and ten, he heard a set of footsteps and then a click. All the lights went out. The footsteps went off into the distance.

Shortly after that, he heard the faraway crash of a heavy door closing, followed by the sound of a car being driven off.

He pulled the hairy blanket away from his face.

It was pitch black.

They were all alone in the museum.

CHAPTER 22

Stuart's flashlight had a wide yellow beam, and April's a narrow bluish one. As they walked through the darkened "Beeton in Wartime" exhibition, their lights criss-crossed, giving sudden eerie glimpses of a figure in a gas mask or a dummy on a stretcher splotched with fake blood.

Stuart nearly walked straight into the waist-height model of 1940s Beeton, and as he lurched over it his flashlight swept across the miniature rooftops and gardens, lighting up something very odd, something that he hadn't noticed before.

"Hey, look—" he started to say, and then he realized that April was hurtling ahead into the next room, flashlight beam bouncing. He hurried after her, past the horse (now back on four legs, with both ears restored), and into the final room.

"Right," she said, ducking under the rope that cordoned off the coin machines. "Which first?" She shined her flashlight between the bicycle tire repair-kit machine and the try-your-strength one.

"The bicycle tire repair machine," he said, fishing in his pocket for the screwdriver.

April watched impatiently as Stuart got to work on the first screw. "Was that a car?" she asked suddenly, cocking her head.

"Didn't hear anything," said Stuart, concentrating hard.

"I hope it wasn't." She sounded anxious. "What if somebody saw our flashlights through the windows? Did you open the one in the bathroom, incidentally?"

"No."

"Why not?"

He shrugged. He was tired of admitting that he was too short to do things. "Didn't have time," he lied.

"What do you mean? You had ages. You had all that time when I was being lectured on those stupid Roman throwing things."

"Yes, but it was complicated."

"What was complicated? How are we going to get out? What if we're stuck in here for the night?"

"Look," he said, feeling exasperated. For all her cleverness, April was an awful worrier. "I'm trying to unscrew this. Why don't you put the money in the fairground machine?"

"Oh, can I?" She sounded thrilled.

"Just to start it up," he said quickly. "I'll do the hammer thing."

"Okay."

He took a threepence out of his other pocket and handed it to her, and then with a couple of twists finished taking out the first screw. "Done it yet?" he asked, starting on the next.

"No . . . not quite. It won't go in."

"Give it a real shove," he said. "I've had to do that on some of the other machines."

The second screw came out quite easily, and the metal strip that covered the coin slot fell to the floor with a tinkle. Stuart pushed a threepence into the slot and pressed a button. There was a metallic clank and a small object landed in the compartment at the bottom. It was oblong, and no wider than his hand. He shoved it, unopened, into his jacket pocket.

"You ready?" he asked, straightening up and shining the flashlight in April's direction. She was crouched over the try-your-strength machine, tugging at something.

"I'm sorry," she said. "I'm really sorry."

"What do you mean?" Stuart shifted the beam of light so that it lit up her hands. Between her fingers, he could see half the threepence sticking out of the slot.

"It's the wrong one," she said.

Stuart leaned over. There were two slots next to each other on the front of the machine. One looked large enough for a threepenny bit. April, for some reason, had stuck the coin into the other, narrower one, meant for sixpences, and it had wedged there.

"Why on earth did you do that?" he asked sharply. He pushed her hands aside and tried to wiggle the coin. It had jammed fast. He inserted the flat end of the screwdriver beside the threepence and moved it around, and the slot started to cave inward. He tugged the coin again and this time it came out.

He held it up and stared at it in the blue flashlight beam. "It's bent," he said accusingly. "You've *bent* it. It's ruined."

April said something, but in a voice so muffled that he couldn't hear the words.

"What's that?" he asked.

"My stupid eyes," she said. "I can't see very well in the dark even with glasses, and the flashlight makes them go all dazzly. I didn't notice the second slot until it was too late. Stupid eyes. Stupid glasses. Stupid, stupid glasses."

He heard her swallow a couple of times and knew that she was trying not to cry. He felt furious, not only with April but also with himself—he'd told her to give the coin a real shove, and that's what she'd done. And then he'd blamed her. It took him a moment or two before he could bring himself to speak.

"I've got another threepence with me," he said, forcing the words out. "It's okay."

She swallowed again. "Look, why don't I go and open the window in the bathroom while you're doing that?" she suggested. "At least I can try and be a bit useful." He heard her footsteps leaving.

"April!" he called out.

"What?"

Stuart took a deep breath. "The window was too high up for me," he said. "But I think you'll be able to reach it."

"Okay." Her footsteps disappeared.

Stuart inspected the try-your-strength machine. It looked straightforward enough. You hit the iron mushroom with a mallet and a small weight was sent whizzing up a vertical groove toward the bell. The mallet looked enormous. He tried to lift it, but it was held in place by a metal catch.

He rested the flashlight on top of the toffee dispenser so that it cast a clear light onto the strength machine and then he pushed threepence into the slot. There was a click as the metal catch fell away. Easing the mallet off its hook, he tried a couple of practice swings and did some deep breathing to get his strength up. "Right," he said to himself.

He took off his jacket, drew another deep breath, lifted the mallet, and at the *exact* moment that he began to swing it, there was a sudden movement in the shadows to his left. Startled, he half turned, and the weight of the mallet threw him off balance, and he staggered back a step and then sat down very hard on the iron mushroom.

It bounced slightly, and there was a pathetic *ding* from the machine. Beside the coin slot, a little drawer shot out of the mechanism. Stuart reached for it, but another hand got there first—a large but slender hand, with polished nails and a bandaged thumb.

"Goodness me," said Jeannie, taking a card the size of a bus ticket out of the drawer. "Whatever is this?"

CHAPTER 23

Stuart's heart seemed to stop. The flashlight rolled off the toffee dispenser and bounced across the floor. For a moment, all was darkness, and then from over his shoulder another flashlight clicked on, illuminating Jeannie. She was standing just in front of him holding the card. On the back of it, in large black letters, was printed the word WEAKLING!

"So tell me," said Jeannie conversationally. "What is the significance of this little object?"

"I don't know," Stuart answered truthfully, his voice not much more than a squeak. "Can I have it back?" he added, reaching out a hand.

"Not yet." She frowned as she read something

on the other side of the card. "It's all very puzzling. And I presume that you've also been interfering with these other machines?"

"No," lied Stuart.

Jeannie stooped into the shadows, and when she straightened up again she was holding his jacket. Stuart made a grab for it. She snatched it out of his reach. "Clifford!" she called.

Stuart looked around and saw the dazzle of a flashlight beam, and then felt his wrists grabbed from behind. Almost immediately they were released again, but now, somehow, he couldn't pull his hands apart; his index fingers seemed to be stuck together behind his back, and the more he struggled the more tightly they were linked.

"That's better," said Jeannie. "Very well done, Clifford. You're well on your way to a distinction in grade two." She lowered Stuart's jacket again, felt in the pockets, and took out the little tin case. "*Top Marks Tire Repair Kit*," she read.

"That's mine," said Stuart.

Jeannie ignored him and opened the lid. "Glue, sandpaper, and a rubber patch," she said, disgustedly.

She snapped the lid shut again. "Where's your little friend?" she asked.

"What friend?"

"The girl with the glasses, who obviously thinks she's rather clever. Wrongly, since it didn't occur to her that Clifford was acting as a rather obvious decoy. I was able to observe your fence-climbing activities at my leisure, and then follow you to the museum in my car. Anyway, where is she?"

"She got scared," Stuart fibbed. "She wanted to go home, so I said okay."

He was feeling scared himself, though he tried not to show it.

"When we met at my factory," said Jeannie, "I distinctly remember asking you to come to me if you found out anything useful about your uncle's workshop. What I *don't* remember saying is, 'Please arrange a secret meeting with Leonora.'"

"It wasn't secret," said Stuart.

"It's the *ingratitude* I can't bear." Jeannie's voice rose in anger. "When I first met that sad old thing, she was trying to sell Grave Street and not getting any buyers because it was a crumbling wreck. Typical teacher, you see—no money, no business acumen. She'd saved nothing for her old age. She didn't have the faintest idea of the true value of what she had."

"What do you mean?" asked Stuart.

"All your great-uncle's early tricks—the bird cage, the money box, the finger trap—were simply collecting dust on her coffee table. Ingenious, beautiful objects left lying around, unpatented. I'm a businesswoman, Stuart. If I see an opportunity, I grasp it. I took the house off Leonora's hands, bought up the old factory site at the bottom of the yard, built a warehouse on it, gave her a lovely rent-free flat in the basement, and began to manufacture your uncle's inventions. The business took off like a rocket. You'd think she'd be grateful, wouldn't you? You'd think she'd be unlikely to sneak off behind my back and give information to a small and nosy boy? I tried to have a conversation with her today, but it wasn't satisfactory. Old people can be so stubborn, and that dog is surprisingly vicious." Broodingly, she rubbed the bandage that covered her thumb. "However," she added, "I have a feeling that *you* might be able to tell me rather more than she did."

Stuart said nothing.

Jeannie leaned toward him so that her face was close to his, and when she spoke again her voice was quiet and reasonable. "Let's be sensible about this," she said. "What would you do with that workshop if you found it? *I* can make use of it. I transformed a few little tricks into an empire of magic. Just think of what I could do with that feast of illusions. No foreign counterfeiters could possibly copy *those*."

She held out the card and the bicycle tire repair kit. "I believe that you're following a trail of some kind, Stuart, and if you can tell me what these objects signify, then I'd be very grateful. And generous—I'd be ever so generous. How about a lovely new bike, for a start?" She smiled.

Stuart shook his head, and her smile disappeared. Jeannie straightened up again, her face rigid, her uninjured hand gripping the card and the little tin. "Let's go, shall we?"

Stuart felt Clifford grasp his shoulders and begin to march him across the room. "Where are you taking me?" he asked, his voice rising.

"No need to shout," said Jeannie. "We're going

somewhere secluded to have a chat about your findings so far."

"Let me go!"

"No."

"My mom and dad'll be worried."

"What a pity. You should have thought of that before you broke into a public building after dark."

Her voice was calm, but there was an edge to it, and Stuart felt his breathing tighten with fear. He tried to shake himself free, but the grip on his shoulders was too strong. One by one—Stuart first, then Clifford, then Jeannie—they passed through the narrow doorway into the room with the tools and farm animals. As the flashlight beam leaped across the walls Stuart saw a shadow move to his left. It was a slow, rather elegant movement, like the spoke of a wheel spinning around, and in an instant he knew what it was. He coughed loudly to cover the thud of a wagon wheel hitting a large fake cow, and then he went boneless, dropping like a stone. Clifford stumbled over him, and there was an exclamation from Jeannie as she banged into the back of her student.

"Oh, for goodness' sake! Now I've dropped that card," she said impatiently. "And please stand up, Stuart. Behaving like a toddler is not going to help you in any—" And then she shrieked as a giant fake blacksmith swooned out of the darkness, a vast hammer in his hand. In the chaos, Stuart found himself momentarily free and he rolled into the deep shadow and staggered to his feet, hands still linked behind his back.

"*Bathroom!*" he heard April hiss. He heard the patter of her feet ahead of him, and her flashlight blinked just once, showing the way to the next room. He followed, zigzagging from one flashlight blink to the next, lurching against exhibits, stumbling through doorways, until April doubled back and took his elbow, dragging him along with her. Stuart could hear the rapid click of Jeannie's heels now, walking swiftly just a room or two behind.

"Here," whispered April, shoving Stuart through the door into the bathroom. "I found a ladder in the janitor's room," she added. "I'll go first."

She scampered up the stepladder to the high window and disappeared. He could hear the thud of her feet hitting the ground outside. Stuart followed, sticking his head and shoulders through the open window and then coming to a halt, his stomach lodged on the windowsill, his feet waving.

April dragged a bin across, climbed on it, grasped the neck of his sweatshirt and pulled. Stuart barely had time to cry out before belly-flopping into a bush. From inside, he heard the crash of the ladder, which he must have kicked over as he fell. April helped haul him to his feet, and then sprinted.

Stuart headed after her, but nearly fell three times in the first hundred yards. "Can't balance. Got to undo my hands," he gasped. He knelt down in the gap between two parked cars and tried to tug his fingers apart.

"Let me see," said April, stopping and crouching beside him. She gave his hands a wrench and he yelled out.

"What are you trying to do, break my fingers?"

"I can't understand it," she said. "There's a shiny metal tube, and you've got a finger in both ends. Just pull."

"I'm pulling."

"Pull harder."

"I can't. It hurts. It—" And then he stopped talking as he heard a noise and saw a light.

Not footsteps, but a siren and the screech of brakes.

Not a flashlight, but the spinning blue lamp of a police car.

CHAPTER 24

"Get under here!" hissed April, crawling beneath the parked van next to them. Stuart wriggled after her, like a caterpillar. From his new viewpoint, his chin an inch or so above the road, he could see the tires of the police car, the door opening, the feet of a policeman getting out. There was a momentary pause, and then another pair of feet, clad in smart high heels, appeared in view.

"Good evening, Officer," came Jeannie's voice.

"Oh, hello, Miss Carr. I didn't expect to see you here." The policeman sounded both surprised and rather respectful. It was as if Jeannie were someone quite important. "We got a call from a local resident who spotted lights in the museum," said the policeman.

"As did I," Jeannie lied. "I was about to call you. I think some vandals must have forced their way in."

"They had trouble yesterday too," said the policeman. "A small boy smashed up the Victorian farm room."

"Shocking," said Jeannie, sounding shocked. "My student Clifford's gone to investigate—shall we join him?"

The two sets of feet disappeared from view.

"We should get out of here," whispered April.

"I still can't move my fingers, they're trapped, they're . . ." *In a trap*, thought Stuart. A Fiendish Finger Trap—and what was it that Leonora had said? *The more you try to free yourself, the firmer you stick. . . .* Instead of pulling he pushed, and instantly the grip loosened. He eased his fingers out, one at a time. "Okay, let's go," he said.

They ran, trying to keep to the side streets, silent apart from their sneakers slapping on the sidewalk. They'd almost reached Beech Road, when April suddenly snorted.

"What's the matter?" asked Stuart, breathless.

She slowed to a stop, doubled over, and snorted again.

"Is it asthma?" asked Stuart.

April shook her head, and he suddenly realized that she was laughing helplessly. "I just can't stop thinking about that blacksmith," she said between snorts. "Waving a hammer at Jeannie. That *was* Jeannie, wasn't it?"

"Yes," said Stuart, glancing around anxiously. The street was empty.

"She just looked like—"April pulled a mad face, and then let out a sort of neigh of laughter.

"*Shhh!*" said Stuart.

"Sorry." She crouched down and took some deep breaths.

"It's serious," said Stuart.

"I know." She looked up at him and made a face again, and he heard himself begin cackling like a nutcase.

It was a minute or two before he managed to speak again. "She took the clues," he said.

"What were they?"

"Well, the first one was a little tin with glue, sandpaper, and a rubber patch inside."

"Did it say anything on the tin?"

"*Top Marks Tire Repair Kit.*"

"Well, that's completely obvious," said April, standing up again, snapping back to her usual organizing self. "When people get top marks they get ten out of ten, don't they? So if the first number of the safe combination is twelve—a dozen toffees in every bag—then the second must be ten. So what's the third?"

"I don't know. A little card came out of the try-your-strength machine, but Jeannie wouldn't let me read it. And then she fell over Clifford and dropped it somewhere."

"So the card might still be in the museum," said April keenly. "We can go and look tomorrow morning. Or, rather, I can go and look, because they'll throw you out if they see you. And if it isn't there, then we can still have a go at the safe. There's only one missing number now, so there's a maximum of twenty-nine combinations we'd have to try and it wouldn't take long to do that.

"Now, your great-uncle's house is being demolished on Monday, so it'll have to be before then. How about tomorrow afternoon? Or evening? Or early Sunday morning? Of course, we'll have to make sure that we're not followed again, but I've just had a really good idea about that. Do you want to hear it?"

Stuart felt exhausted. Didn't she ever stop bossing people around? "Not right this second," he said a bit grumpily. "Tomorrow will do. We've got the whole weekend."

"Oh." She looked disappointed. "Okay. It is pretty late, I suppose. We ought to be getting home."

They jogged back to where they'd hidden the kitchen stool and quickly scaled the six fences between the alleyway and Stuart's backyard.

"Okay," said Stuart. "Bye, then." He had almost reached the back door when two things occurred to him. The first was that his parents would be expecting him to come in by the *front* door, and the second was that April had invented the plan, got him into the museum, saved him from Jeannie, and then got him safely out again.

"April!" he called.

"Yes?"

"Thanks."

"That's all right."

"And, April?"

"Yes?"

"My mom and dad will be expecting me in by the front door."

"Just tell them you climbed over our back fence for fun," said April.

"Oh. Okay." She really was irritatingly clever.

He let himself into the house, shouted "hello" to his parents, and then opened the fridge and started to eat everything that wasn't either raw or made of vegetables.

It wasn't until he was lying in bed that he started to think about the clues again. Something kept nagging away at the back of his mind, something about the toffee machine. Or was it about the bingo hall? Or was it about that old lady who'd been dressed entirely in blue? If only someone would stop saying,

"Stuart, wake up," in his ear, then he'd be able to remember what it was.

"Stuart, wake up!" said the voice again.

He opened his eyes. Light was creeping around the edge of the curtains and his mother was standing beside his bed, fully dressed.

His father's head appeared over her shoulder. "Dawn salutations to our esteemed offspring!" he said. His father had a hat on. The straw hat that he only ever wore on vacation.

"What's happening?" asked Stuart.

His mother sat on the edge of the bed and ruffled his hair. "We've not spent much time as a family lately," she said, "and I'm sorry. I think it's been pretty miserable for you, moving to a new town and not knowing anybody. You've not been your old self. So we thought we should have a long weekend away and do something lovely together. I spent all yesterday arranging it as a surprise."

"A long weekend?" repeated Stuart, struggling to understand. "So you mean we won't get back to Beeton until . . .?"

"Monday lunchtime," said his mother. "So get

dressed, have a quick breakfast, and we're off! The taxi comes in half an hour."

"By noon we shall be breathing West Country air," added his father unhelpfully.

They closed the door and left Stuart sitting open-mouthed.

The house, he thought.

Great-Uncle Tony's house is going to be knocked down on Monday morning.

CHAPTER 25

Stuart got dressed so fast that he put his T-shirt on inside out, and then he galloped down the stairs and opened the front door. He ran onto the sidewalk barefoot and looked up at April's house. Every curtain was closed. He picked up a pebble to throw at the window and then hesitated. What if he woke up the wrong triplet?

He dashed back into the house, grabbed some paper, and then for a moment he hesitated with the pen in his hand. This had been *his* adventure, *his* great-uncle, *his* clues, *his* inheritance. Could he really bear to hand it over to someone else? And then he thought of Leonora, who had been waiting for fifty years to find out what had happened to her sister. And he wrote:

DEAR APRIL,
TERRIBLE NEWS. MY PARENTS
TOOK ME AWAY FOR THE
WEEKEND, WON'T BE BACK TILL
MONDAY LUNCH TIME. CAN YOU
OPEN THE SAFE, PLEASE?
GOOD LUCK.

STUART

He put the note in an envelope marked *April* and slid it through the mail slot in her front door.

And then he went on vacation.

When other people's parents said they were going to spend a family weekend doing "something lovely," they usually meant they were going to the beach, or to Alton Towers, or to Disneyland. Stuart's parents' idea of "something lovely" was a camping weekend in Wiltshire, in which the days were spent going on very long hikes carrying knapsacks full of egg sandwiches, and the evenings meant lying in a tent listening to the radio, or squinting at books by flashlight. The walks were largely educational.

"An Iron Age fort," said Stuart's mother delightedly, as yet another vague, grass-covered lump came into view. "And the map shows there's a neolithic tomb only a couple of miles away. That'll be exciting, won't it?"

"Mmm," said Stuart, who was spending most of the time tensely wondering how April was getting on. Though, as he kept reminding himself, if anyone was capable of getting into a condemned house and opening a locked safe, it was April. In fact, the more he thought about it, the more certain he was that she'd succeed. He couldn't imagine that she'd ever failed at *anything*.

The neolithic tomb was, at least, pleasantly spooky. It was a large round mound, with a dark entrance down a narrow set of stone steps. At the bottom, the opening widened into a circular room, from which three stone passages radiated. Stuart stood in the center and slowly shone his flashlight beam around the space. He had the oddest feeling that he'd seen it before—but it had been smaller, and he'd seen it from *above*.

He shut his eyes for a moment, and remembered that night in the museum, when he had nearly walked smack into the model of wartime Beeton. His light beam had flashed across the miniature town, and for the briefest of moments he had seen a trio of tunnels—air-raid shelters—converging on a wide central area, just like the one that he was now standing in. That central area had been just beneath a delicate little raised structure with a pointed roof. At the time, he hadn't recognized it, but now he suddenly knew what it was: the bandstand. The bandstand in the park! It had never occurred to him that there might be something *underneath* it. And if there was, then there had to be an entrance that he'd missed.

He thought of the last photograph in the book. Uncle Tony had been sitting on the grass next to a poster that read SUNDAY CONCERTS.

A poster on a bulletin board.

A bulletin board screwed to the base of the bandstand.

"It's *behind* it!" he shouted. And from the stone walls, his voice boomed back at him: *behind, behind, behind.*

His father looked up from the leaflet he was reading and said, "Did you know that the word *echo* comes from the Greek legend about a nymph?"

"Nope," said Stuart, and he had a mad urge to run all the way back to Beeton to share the news with April. But there was still another whole day of the vacation to go, and the time seemed to pass with unbearable slowness.

Sunday afternoon was spent slogging up a steep and winding hill, to look at the view (fields, mainly), and in the evening the camping stove kept blowing out, so they ate cold soup and rolls and listened to a radio play about Irish potato farmers.

Monday morning came at last. They caught an early bus to the train station, bought five newspapers so that Stuart's father could check out the crosswords, and stood waiting for the 8:55 to Beeton. It was late.

"Here's one to pass the time," said his father. "*Raise fig to model present*. Four letters."

"Don't know," said Stuart.

"Gift," declared Mr. Horten. "It's *fig* backward, you see, and then T, as in Model T Ford."

"You're looking at your watch a lot, Stuart," said his mother. "Is there something you need to get back for?"

"I just want to see April."

"One of the girls next door?"

He nodded.

"Oh, but it's *so lovely* that you've made such a good friend already," said his mother, and she gave him an embarrassingly public hug.

"Try this one," his father offered, rustling *The Times*. "*Breadmaker's quantity unlucky for the trisketaphobic*. Eight letters."

"Don't know," said Stuart.

"It's rather straightforward. Trisketaphobia is a fear of the number thirteen, and '*breadmaker's quantity*' refers to the phrase 'a baker's dozen,' which, of course, also means thirteen."

"Here's the train," said his mother.

But Stuart had stopped looking along the track and was staring, horrified, up at his father. "Thirteen?" he repeated. "A baker's dozen means thirteen?"

His father nodded enthusiastically. "The phrase is believed to originate from the medieval practice of adding an extra loaf to the . . ."

But Stuart had stopped listening. Instead, he was thinking of the bingo hall and of the old ladies who'd talked to him in the foyer. "*Baker's dozen,*" Vi had said of the number of toffees in every bag. "*Unluckily for my teeth,*" Lorna had added, but Stuart had missed that extra clue and had just assumed that the baker's bit was the name of a sort of toffee. All he had remembered was the word *dozen*. He'd told April that the first number of the safe combination must be twelve, but he'd been wrong. Horribly, ignorantly, wrong.

CHAPTER 26

He sat on the train, rigid with disbelief. How long would April have spent trying, hopelessly, to open the safe? *She* would have known what a baker's dozen was . . .

A thin drizzle began to streak the windows.

"Nearly there," said his mother, as the rain grew heavier.

It was torrential by the time they arrived in Beeton. The taxi from the train station felt more like a boat, swishing through the puddles.

"Who's that?" asked his mother, pressing her face to the window as they drew into Beech Road. The rain was like a flapping gray curtain, and through it

Stuart could just see a small figure leaning out of a window of the triplets' house, binoculars to eyes. A second later, the figure disappeared.

The taxi stopped and Stuart opened the door. As he did so, the front door of the triplets' house flew open and April shot out and ran over, shouting something frantically.

"What?" asked Stuart.

"Now!" screeched April, grabbing him by the arm and pulling him from the car. "You have to go right now! *Right now!!!!*"

"Go where?" Stuart was bewildered. He'd only been out of the car for five seconds and he was already soaked. The rain was streaming down April's glasses and dripping off the bottom of the frames.

"Your great-uncle Tony's house," said April.

"You mean it's still there?" He'd assumed it would be just a pile of rubble by now.

"It might be still there," said April. "It might just possibly. April promised to try and stop it, but I don't know whether she's managed."

"What?" asked Stuart, feeling and sounding stupid.

"April promised to try and stop it," said April, loudly and clearly.

"But you're April," he said. "Aren't you?"

She shook her head. "I'm May. I'm wearing April's glasses. She didn't want to be followed, so she went disguised."

"Disguised as who?"

"As *me*, you idiot."

Stuart shook his head. He felt as if the rain had leaked into his ears.

"Just *listen*," said May, leaning close and shoving a pink plastic purse into his hand. "She told me to tell you that she tried to do whatever it was that you wanted her to do, but she couldn't. The numbers wouldn't work, so she's gone to try and stop the demolition; she said to give you this purse. She found the card underneath a cow, she said. And she told me to look for you, and to send you over *as soon as* you got here. Not after half an hour of you saying, 'What?' to everything I tell you."

"Okay, okay, okay," said Stuart thinking, yet again, what an infuriating trio they were. "But I'll be followed, too," he added.

May shook her head. "June put on April's spare glasses and went off to the swimming pool two hours ago. They'll be following her."

"Right. I'll get going then." He felt a bit stunned by the complexity of the plan. "So how much did April tell you about Great-Uncle Tony and the house and everything?" he asked as he turned to leave.

May shook her head, raindrops spraying from her glasses. "Nothing," she said. "She never tells us anything. She's the quiet one of the family."

Stuart's parents had been watching him from the open door of the house, and now he ran up to them and gabbled, "Gotta go right away gotta see one of the triplets I'll be careful won't talk to any strangers be careful crossing the road I'll be back for tea." Then he ran off, returning briefly to grab the raincoat that his mother was waving at him.

His feet sent up great sprays of water from the wet sidewalk, and he swerved past pedestrians and skidded around corners, reaching the corner of Great-Uncle Tony's street in only five minutes. He stopped dead. Because there, in front of the house, parked over the smashed remains of the fence and gate, was a huge yellow machine. It had tank tracks, a cab with a high seat, and a vast hydraulic arm. At the end of the arm was a colossal pair of toothed metal jaws that had already taken four or five savage bites out of the roof and gutters of the house. The attic beams were visible, the broken ends as pale as straw, and the yard was filled with shattered shingles. But the jaws were no longer moving, and the cab was empty. A cluster of workmen, all wearing hard hats, were staring up at the hydraulic arm, and staring back down at them from the very top of it, was April.

She was sitting, legs dangling, arms folded, a good twenty feet above the ground. As Stuart watched, one of the workmen threw down his hat in frustration and started to climb up the side of the cab.

Instantly, April scrambled to her feet, closed her eyes, and stood on one leg. All the workmen shouted "*No!*" and the one who'd been climbing up the cab leaped back off. April opened her eyes, lowered her foot, and carefully sat back down again.

Stuart had been standing as if nailed to the ground, but now he managed to unstick himself and began to creep forward. The men had their backs to him. He raised his hand and gave a tiny, subtle wave to April. She ignored him. He gave a larger wave, but she still took no notice and then he realized that without her glasses, he was probably nothing more than a blur. He waved both hands, and then both arms, and then he jumped up and down, thankful that the rain would blot out any noise.

At last April seemed to spot him. She squinted in his direction and then deliberately looked away, and scratched her head. But the hand that was doing the scratching had one finger sticking out, and it pointed in the direction of the house.

"April!" shouted the oldest of the group of men. "If you don't come down right now, you will spend your birthday locked in the spare room, while your sisters have a huge party. And their present will be a trip to Disneyland. Without you."

"Don't care, Dad," said April. She began to whistle tunelessly.

Stuart tiptoed across the broken fence, passed behind the group of men, and ran down the alleyway along the side of the house. The back door was open. Stuart walked cautiously in through the kitchen and along the corridor. The long room was now empty of furniture, and the walls were patterned with sliding rain shadows. In the rippling gray light, he opened the little purse that May had given him and took out a folded note and a dusty piece of card the size of a bus ticket. On one side (the side he'd seen before) it said:

WEAKLING!

And on the other:

YOU'LL NEED TO DOUBLE YOUR EFFORTS
TO GET THE RIGHT RESULT!

Hurriedly, Stuart unfolded the note. It was written in a horrible, hasty scrawl.

Museum was closed Sat, being dusted for
vandal's fingerprints, so I went to Unc Tony's
house anyway and tried 12, 10 and every

*possible last number—didn't work. Went back
to museum first thing this morning, found
this card. It's obviously an instruction, not
a number. I haven't had time to try it.
Sorry to let you down. Will try and delay
the demolition . . .*

Faintly, from the front yard Stuart could
hear April's father threatening to phone the fire
department. There was no more time for fooling
around. He had to get the combination right the
first time. He closed his eyes and thought.

Thirteen toffees.

Top Marks Tire Repair Kit. (Ten out of ten.)

An instruction to double his efforts.

He opened his eyes again, lifted the picture from
the wall, and grasped the little dial.

He turned it clockwise to 26, counterclockwise
to 20, and clockwise all the way around to 20 again.
There was a sharp *click*, and the door jerked in his
grasp. He pulled, and it swung open.

For a moment he thought it was empty, and then
Stuart put in his hand and felt around, patting the

darkness. There, in one corner, his fingers touched a small, flat object. A key. A key far too small for any door. A *padlock* key.

He closed his fist around it and was back out of the house in seconds.

In the front garden, April's father was still shouting. "And your sisters will also be getting new bikes. And a hundred dollars to spend on clothes. And . . . and a *horse* each!"

April had put her fingers in her ears.

Stuart sneaked back to the sidewalk, but the rain had eased off, and there was nothing to cover the sound of the broken fence rocking under his feet.

"What are you doing?" asked one of the men, swinging around.

"Nothing," said Stuart. "Just watching." He stuck his hands in his pockets and tried to look casual.

". . . and a trip to London. Without you!" called April's father. "Madame Tussaud's, Leicester Square, the—"

"Okay, Dad, I'll come down," said April.

"*What?*" Her father gaped up at her, but she was already sliding back along the hydraulic arm. She landed neatly on both feet on the roof of the cab, and scrambled quickly down the outside of it to the ground.

"Sorry, Dad," she said, looking up at her father meekly.

He looked too stunned, or too furious, to speak.

"Sorry, Dad," she repeated. "But there was a really good reason for it. Sorry, everyone. Really sorry." And then she ran, and Stuart ran with her.

"Are you going to be in trouble?" he asked her breathlessly, as they galloped along the sidewalk.

"Massive trouble," she gasped. "*Massive.* Probably no spending money for a year. Probably washing the dishes until I'm eighteen. Here . . ."

She veered toward a house that they were passing. It had a weeping-willow tree planted in the front yard, with leafy branches hanging thickly to the ground. She pushed through the rustling curtain, and Stuart followed her.

"We've used this before for secret meetings," she said. "No one can see us from the street."

It was as if they were standing in a green cave.

"That was a fantastic thing you did," he said.

April shrugged. "Glad it worked. But did you get the safe open?"

He nodded and opened his fist, and they both peered at the small key.

"What's it for?" she asked.

Stuart grinned triumphantly. "The entrance to the workshop," he said. "And I think I know where to look for it."

CHAPTER 27

"The trouble with the bandstand," said April, "is that if Jeannie follows us, there's nowhere to hide. You can't sneak there without being spotted."

It was the next morning and they were in the bedroom that April shared with her sisters, a large-scale map of Beeton spread across the floor in front of them. Stuart had marked the bandstand with a dot of black ink, and all around it were the broad green acres of the park.

"If we went after dark—" began Stuart.

April shook her head. "I'm not allowed out anywhere in the evening for about a thousand years," she said. "That's one part of the punishment."

They were silent for a while, staring at the map. "I wonder—" began April, and then a bell rang from somewhere downstairs, and she got up with a groan. "I won't be long."

She was gone for ten minutes, and when she came back she smelled strongly of shoe polish.

"Dad needed his work boots cleaned," she told Stuart gloomily. "That's the *other* part of the punishment. For the next month, whenever Mom or Dad needs a job done, they ring that bell, and I have to run. So, have you had any ideas?"

"No," said Stuart.

"It's a pity there aren't a few bushes around the bandstand. We could camouflage ourselves like soldiers, put green paint on our faces and leaves in our—"

The bell rang again. April rolled her eyes and left the room.

Stuart stood up and stretched, and wandered over to the girls' desk. Stuck to the wall above it was a photo of the three of them looking ridiculously serious, with the words NEWS TEAM printed underneath. The latest edition of the *Beech*

Road Guardian was still on the printer beside the computer and he glanced at the front page.

EXCITING LINE-UP FOR
BEETON SUMMER FESTIVAL

A thrilling day of exciting activities awaits the inhabitants of Beeton, beginning with an outdoor children's talent show, to be judged by the lady mayoress, and ending with a parade of decorated floats along Main Street.

For an EXCLUSIVE interview with the lady mayoress, conducted by June Kingley, with photographs by May Kingley, see page 2.

For a detailed timetable of the day's events, see page 4.

Stuart turned to the back page of the newspaper and began to read idly.

"Sorry," said April, opening the door. "I just had to empty the compost bin. What are you looking at?"

"This," said Stuart, holding up the paper.

She shrugged. "I don't work on it any more. Much too dull."

"No, I mean, *this*!" He jabbed a finger at the timetable on the back page. "There's a children's talent contest the day after tomorrow. And they're holding it at the bandstand!"

April made a face. "So? There'll be a million kids there. That's no good."

Stuart shook his head. "You're wrong," he said. "It'll be perfect. In a crowd of a million kids, who's going to notice two extra?"

There were big kids. Small kids. Tiny kids. Kids dressed as superheroes, kids with pink plastic guitars, kids with juggling balls, kids in ballet shoes, and one kid with a parrot that kept shouting,

"HELLO THERE!" in a Welsh accent. The sky was blue, the sun was shining, and the park was absolutely, completely, totally full.

With painful slowness, Stuart and April edged their way toward the bandstand, where a small girl was singing "Somewhere Over the Rainbow" while accompanying herself on a miniature drum kit.

There were a few dozen rows of seats and a table for the judges, but nearly everyone else in the crowd was standing, craning for a better view, taking photographs.

"Excuse me," said Stuart to a large woman. She had a double baby carriage and was rocking it rather violently, trying to quiet a pair of wailing twins.

"Excuse me," he said again.

She frowned down at him. "You should have gotten here earlier if you wanted a good view. You can't just shove your way to the front like that." She rocked the twins harder, ignoring him.

Stuart looked around at April, who was carrying a folding chair. "She won't let me past," he muttered.

"Start panting," ordered April.

"What?"

"Just do it. *Pant.*"

He panted.

"Can you let us through?" said April loudly. "My little brother's having a panic attack. Let us through, please!"

The crowd parted.

"Thank you," said April, squeezing through the gap.

Stuart followed her, still panting, avoiding the pitying looks. He could feel himself going crimson with the humiliation. "You didn't have to say 'little brother,'" he hissed crossly.

"WHAT?" asked April. The drum solo was incredibly loud.

"Oh, never mind." He forced himself to concentrate. The base of the bandstand was just ahead, the bulletin board now visible through the thicket of legs. As he reached it, he dropped to a crouch and unslung the bag he'd brought with him. As planned, April stood in front, using the folding chair to screen him from view.

The board was about three feet square and bolted to the brickwork. This time Stuart had come prepared with a backpack full of tools borrowed from April's father's garden shed. The first bolt came out fairly easily.

"WON'T BE LONG!" he shouted to April, just as "Somewhere Over the Rainbow" came to a noisy end. The applause went on for what felt like minutes. Stuart took out another two bolts.

"*Thank you, little Dora Moffatt!*" said a hugely amplified voice. "*We now realize that all that was missing from* The Wizard of Oz *was a prolonged drum solo! What did our panel think of it? Ah, yes, I can see the lady mayoress giving the thumbs up. And next up is a tap-dance troop. Let's hear it for the Beeton Beat!*" There was more applause, and then the rattle of tap shoes and the rumble of a giant sound system belting out "Thriller."

"LAST ONE!" yelled Stuart. He checked over his shoulder, but all he could see was people's legs. No one was spying. No one even knew he and April were there. He checked in his pocket. He had the key and he had the last two threepences, one intact and one bent. He was ready.

As he took out the final bolt, the bulletin board

fell forward, and he caught it, laying it to one side.

Behind it was a small, square metal hatch, hinged at the bottom and fastened with a padlock at the top. Quickly Stuart used the key, and the padlock sprang open. He pulled at the handle. The hatch stayed closed. He pulled again and it opened about an inch. Flakes of rust fluttered onto his fingers.

"What's the matter?" asked April, peering down.

"I think it's rusted shut," he said. He pulled, and pulled again, and then stood up and used his foot. Then April tried too, and with a horrible screech the door opened halfway before sticking there, immovably.

Stuart crouched down again and took a flashlight out of his bag. Shoving his head and shoulders through the gap, he shone it into the darkness. Directly below the hatch, a metal ladder spanned the gap to the floor, ten feet below. Beyond it, a huge circular room opened out below ground level.

"What can you see?" asked April.

Stuart moved the flashlight beam around and felt his breath catch and his eyes grow wide. "Wonderful things!" he said.

CHAPTER 28

It was a very tight squeeze, getting through the hatch and onto the ladder. As Stuart descended, April peered down at him, her head framed by the narrow opening.

"I won't be able to get through," she called despairingly. "I'm too big."

"I won't be long," said Stuart. He realized that he was grinning.

As he climbed down into the void, the music grew muffled, but the noise of the tap dancers became even louder. It was like being on the inside of a drum.

He stepped off the ladder and switched on

his flashlight. The huge circular room was brick-walled. In the center, a series of tapering iron pillars supported the floor of the bandstand overhead. Outside the circle of pillars lay his uncle's workshop. He could see a hoist and a workbench, a lathe, a vice, and a rack of tools. But it was not those that had made his eyes widen.

Slowly he walked around the circumference of the room, and his flashlight beam caught and flashed on one object after another—a golden pyramid, taller than himself; a bronze throne, entwined with silver wire and enameled flowers; a giant fan, iridescent as a peacock's tail; a graceful mirrored arch that sent the flashlight beam bouncing back to him, endlessly multiplied.

Fascinated by the reflections, he moved closer to the arch and saw dozens and dozens of Stuarts . . .

"WHAT HAVE YOU FOUND?" called April through the hatch.

"TELL YOU IN A MINUTE!" he shouted back.

An oval cabinet came next, pierced by a cluster of gold-handled swords, and after that a giant book propped up against the wall, the jet-black cover locked by a huge key, the words OPEN AT YOUR PERIL picked out in letters of red and silver.

And then another object caught in the flashlight beam, and though Stuart had never seen it before he knew exactly what it was. Mesmerized, he walked toward it: the Well of Wishes.

Not a little pixie well with a wobbly bucket and a quaint tiled roof, but something strange and more beautiful, the cold color of moonlight, dusted with stars. A well filled not with water but with silvery shadow.

And as the tap dancers thundered overhead, Stuart stared at the shimmering darkness. Great-Uncle Tony had stood just here. He had wished for his heart's desire and he had thrown in a coin, and then . . . what? Where had he gone? Why hadn't he ever returned?

Stuart felt curiosity seize him so strongly that it was like a hook drawing him onward. He had only half believed before, but he had no doubt now that there was real magic in this place; there was a weight to it, a thickness in the air. He reached into his pocket and took out the last two threepences. They felt heavy in his palm.

The world seemed suddenly limitless. He could wish for anything, he realized, anything at all. He could wish for his *own* heart's desire.

He could wish to be taller.

Because life would be so much better, so much easier if he could just be the same height as other ten-year-olds. No one would pass him off as a younger brother, no one would call him "little chap." He wouldn't get patted on the head or offered books of stickers or junior backpacks to keep him quiet in museums. He wouldn't have to avoid telling people his last name. He'd never get called "Shorty Shorten" again . . .

Or perhaps he could be more ambitious with his wish.

Rather than taller, why not *tall*?

Why not be the one in the class who could reach everything, the one who got stopped on buses because he looked too old to travel on a children's ticket, the one who got picked first for sports, the one who got called "Shorty" just as a joke, not as a description? He imagined having to look down at April and her sisters, leaning his elbow on the fence, laughing at their astonishment when he told them his age.

"*Honestly, I'm ten.*"

"*You can't be.*"

"*No, I am.*"

And he wouldn't have to dread starting his new school in the fall. He wouldn't have his mom and dad *worrying* about him all the time.

He drew a long breath and looked at the coins in his palm.

Was it possible?

Could he change his whole life in a second? Could he alter something so fundamental?

And he felt his insides curl in fear, because the idea was both thrilling and terrifying. He clenched his hand around the coins, and then slowly, slowly, he leaned over the well . . .

"YO, STUART!" shouted April from the hatch. "CAN YOU PLEASE, *PLEASE* FIND ANOTHER WAY FOR ME TO GET IN? I'M DESPERATE TO SEE WHAT'S IN THERE."

Stuart took a step back and gulped in air, as if he'd come up from a long dive underwater, and then he pushed the threepences back into his pocket. There would be time later. He had found the workshop now. He had beaten Jeannie to the prize; there was no longer any hurry. From outside, he could hear "Thriller" reaching its thunderous climax.

"ALL RIGHT!" he shouted, stirring himself. On his way around the room, he knew he'd seen two doors, and he went back to look at them. They were identical: set deeply in the wall, almost opposite each other, and firmly shut, with no obvious keyholes. They reminded him vaguely of the doors in a ship.

And halfway between the doors, fixed to the brickwork, there was a metal wheel, three feet across. It had spokes, like a ship's wheel. A ship's doors; a ship's wheel. If he turned it, then the doors might open. It had to be worth trying.

Distantly, over the applause, Stuart could hear the tinny voice of the emcee. "*And now, as a complete contrast, we have a group of budding ballerinas. Let's hear it for Beeton's Ballet Babes in the 'Dance of the Sugar Plum Fairy.'*"

A hideous tinkling tune filtered down through the hatch.

He stuck his flashlight in his back pocket, gripped the wheel, and tried to turn it. He dragged at the spokes until he could feel his face turning red, but it didn't budge. It must be rusted shut, like the hatch, he thought, and he was just about to shout up at April, when an idea occurred to him. He reached out, gripped the spokes again and turned the wheel the *other* way, counterclockwise. It spun sweetly in his hands, just as the lid of the money box had done all those days ago.

Stuart laughed, and looked across at one of the doors to watch it as it opened, but it was still firmly shut, and then the tinkly music stopped with a horrible burst of static. A small girl screamed, and then a whole load of small girls screamed.

From behind him came a clanking, wheezing noise, and Stuart turned to see a curved crack of light appearing in the ceiling. The tapered pillars were telescoping into themselves. *The whole circular floor of the bandstand above him was slowly dropping down, like an elevator descending!*

Stuart watched, frozen, as it sank. A group of pink-clad ballet dancers, all about six years old, were huddled in the center of the stage, arms around one another, screaming wildly. Sunlight flooded into the workshop. A ring of faces appeared over the railing at the top, staring downward, their mouths open in horror.

The pillars grew shorter, and with a hiss and a shudder the stage reached the ground, a few feet in front of Stuart.

The ballet dancers clustered in a terrified group, looking upward. Mothers were wailing, cameras were flashing, a distant siren grew gradually nearer.

Suddenly a clear, crisp, female voice spoke over the loudspeaker, cutting through the chaos. "*There is no need to panic. No one appears to be injured. A fire engine is on its way. I can assure everyone that this situation is entirely under control. Please stay calm.*"

The ring of faces at the top had all turned to look at the speaker, and now they clustered together to make room as she appeared at the railing. It was the lady mayoress, microphone in hand. She was wearing a fur-edged red robe, a dark hat, and a heavy gold chain of office—but it was her face that Stuart goggled up at, scarcely able to believe his eyes.

A sharp, bright-eyed face.

It was Jeannie.

CHAPTER 29

Jeannie peered over the railing, and her gaze swept across the room beneath the bandstand. Stuart ducked into the shadows, but he could still see her slow, triumphant smile.

"*As your mayoress,*" she continued, raising the microphone again, "*I give you my word that as soon as these talented young performers have been safely rescued, this entire area will be sealed off and I shall personally work night and day to investigate the incident, and to clear out any dangerous machinery and other items that may have been exposed by the subsidence of the bandstand floor.*"

"Oh, I bet you will," muttered Stuart. He felt as if

he'd been knocked sideways. All that planning and thinking and hunting and hiding, and now Jeannie was ready to whisk in and take everything away. He gnawed at a fingernail, his mind blank apart from one sure and certain thought: April would know what to do.

He looked across at the ladder. Could he creep over and hope that the sugar plum fairies wouldn't notice him?

"Look, there's a *ladder*!" shrieked one of the ballet dancers at that very moment. Terror forgotten, she scampered across to it and began to climb.

Stuart saw April's anxious face darting out of sight at the top. The rest of the Beeton Ballet Babes formed a giggling line at the bottom.

Well, that's that, thought Stuart.

He stared at the two doors again, but they were still shut. And then he frowned. Why only *two* doors? Both the model in the museum and the neolithic tomb had had *three* entrances to the underground room: three entrances, evenly spaced. He looked from one door to the other, and then he let his eyes travel the same distance again along the curving wall. Where they rested he saw, not a door, but the giant book, leaning against the wall.

OPEN AT YOUR PERIL

The cover was deepest black, but he could see the glint of the key.

Crouching, he inched around the circumference of the room. The last two ballet dancers were lining up for the ladder. Jeannie had disappeared from view.

As the last dancer began to climb, Stuart sprinted across to the book, turned the key, and then tried to lift the cover. It was heavy, but he heaved it open a few inches and peered in. It took a moment for his eyes to adjust to the darkness, but then he saw a dull reflection of his own face and realized that the cover concealed not a doorway but a cabinet with a metal back.

A loud noise made him turn. The last dancer had disappeared through the hatch, but now a series of thuds were coming from the same place, and a shower of rust flakes caught the light as they fluttered to the floor. With a screech of metal, the door of the hatch opened fully, and a smartly shod foot came through the gap and groped for the rung of the ladder. The foot belonged to a woman. Stuart hesitated just long enough to see the bottom of a fur-edged mayoral robe, and then he squeezed through the narrow opening into the book. He tried to keep the door very slightly open, but there was nothing to grip, and it closed behind him with a sharp *click*. There was an instant of suffocating panic, and then the back of the cabinet swung open and Stuart sprawled into darkness.

His head hurt, and for a long time he didn't feel properly awake. And when he did wake, there was no light at all, so that he wasn't even sure whether his eyes were open or not. He lifted a hand and felt a lump on the side of his head, where he must have hit it on the ground as he fell. He'd been lying on the floor knocked out, he realized.

He sat up, slowly and carefully, and then—

suddenly fearful—checked in his back pocket for the flashlight. It was gone. He patted the floor all around him but felt nothing but a fine layer of grit. He moved his arms in a wide circle, and found that at fullest stretch he could just touch a wall on either side.

Cautiously, he stood up. The ceiling was high, too high for him to reach. He started to walk forward, arms extended in front of him. He'd only taken a couple of steps when his foot caught something that rolled across the floor and he pounced down (quite a slow pounce, given the pain in his head) and scrambled after the object. His fingers closed over a small metal cylinder, and he let out a squawk of joy. It was his flashlight!

He turned it on. Immediately ahead was a metal door. There was no handle, just a pair of jointed rods at the top and two large springs at the bottom. It was firmly closed. Through the fog that seemed to fill his head, he tried to think.

It was the book, he realized. He was looking at the back of the OPEN AT YOUR PERIL book. It was a stage illusion, a disappearing trick, with a back door that opened when the front cover was closed. And presumably, the reverse was true: the back was now closed which meant that someone must have opened the front cover.

Jeannie, he thought. *Jeannie's inspecting the workshop.*

Hastily, he turned around and shone the flashlight in the other direction. A long, straight tunnel stretched away, the walls featureless, the floor thick with wooly dust. Stuart began to walk, and the dust rose in soft clouds and drifted like sparks across the flashlight beam.

He kept walking; the only noise his own muffled footsteps. He wondered how much time had passed since he'd shut himself in the book. Had he been lying on the floor for hours or only minutes? He plunged a hand into his pocket to check that he still had the final two threepences, and the coins chinked in his hand. He felt a jolt of regret. He should have made a wish when he had the chance; he had hesitated and now the moment had gone . . .

He was shaken from his thoughts by a fork in the tunnel. He shone his flashlight beam to the right and saw nothing but a continuation of the corridor. Then he shone it to the left. Oddly, a heavy curtain blocked the way. Stuart started to lift it aside, but there was a soft ripping noise and the whole thing fell to the ground in a flurry of moths.

Behind it was a face. Stuart screamed.

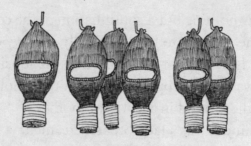

CHAPTER 30

The face hung in the darkness, swinging gently: a single oval eye, a flat snout, the skin an oily green. Behind it hung a row of identical faces, all twisting slowly in the drafts.

In a second, before he had even taken another breath, Stuart realized what they were. *Gas masks,* he thought, and then he said the words out loud, because it was reassuring to hear his own voice. "Second World War gas masks."

He moved the flashlight beam and saw an arrow on the wall, and the words AIR-RAID SHELTER. A few feet beyond it, the tunnel widened into a sort of cave, and the space was filled with rows of benches.

Stuart was still breathless from the shock, and his legs felt weightless and feeble, as if they were made of string. He wobbled over to one of the benches and sat down. He shone his flashlight beam at the floor, because he didn't enjoy watching those sightless masks all quietly swinging, and he recited the five-times table to himself, just to steady his thoughts.

A daddy-longlegs scuttled across the flashlight beam, and then the pool of light between his feet began to flicker rapidly. Stuart turned the flashlight off and on again. For a second or two it shone more brightly than before, and then the yellow light dwindled to an orange glimmer, before blinking out completely.

He sat in the utter darkness, more afraid than he'd ever been before, and the only thing he could think to do was to carry on reciting the five-times table. When he'd finished that, he moved on to sixes, and then on to sevens, and he was just starting on eights when he heard a noise. It was such an incongruous noise here in these dusty, forgotten tunnels that for a moment he couldn't believe his ears, and then it happened again. It was the sound of a dog, barking. There were footsteps as well, and a sudden, welcome blur of bluish light. He heard a voice that he recognized.

"April!" he shouted, standing up. And there, coming along the tunnel toward him, was April—and Leonora and the guide dog, Pluto. It gave another little "*woof*" when it saw Stuart, and April screeched with surprise and ran forward, half throttling him with a hug.

"How did you get here?" he asked, when he'd managed to disentangle himself. "And how come you're with Leonora, and how long have I been down here, anyway?"

"A couple of hours. Maybe three," April told him. "And you won't believe what happened. You see, I saw Jeannie climb down the ladder—"

"I'm sorry to interrupt," said Leonora calmly, "but Stuart sounds to me as if he might need a little energy boost. We have snacks."

"Fantastic!" said Stuart. "There are benches here," he added for Leonora's benefit, and they all sat down to the oddest picnic he'd ever had, eating shrimp-cocktail flavored potato chips by flashlight, with the row of gas masks swaying overhead.

"As I was saying," gabbled April, after Stuart had told his own story. "I saw Jeannie go down the ladder, and I was going to follow her, but then the firefighters came and shooed everyone away and closed the park, and then the police turned up too, and someone from the local TV news as well, and I didn't know what to do. I thought you were probably hiding down there, so I hung around for a while to see if you'd sneak out, and then when you didn't, I started to get really worried. I remembered you'd said there were *underground* entrances to the workshop, so I went back to the museum and looked at the model and there were three different tunnels to the room under the bandstand."

"I know," said Stuart. "I fell into one of them and hit my head."

"And the tunnels came out in different bits of the town—they were all used as air-raid shelters. One came out under Beeton police station, so I knew I couldn't get in there. And one was labeled DISUSED DUE TO FLOODING IN 1941, so I knew that was no good. The third came out into the basement of Saint Cuthbert's Teacher-training College. But there *isn't* a teacher-training college in Beeton—at least, not anymore. And then I had a brilliant thought—"

"There was a ring at my door," interrupted Leonora, smiling. "And when I answered it, I heard a young voice say, 'You don't know me, but you know my friend Stuart, and *he* said that you trained as a teacher in Beeton, ages ago. So can you tell me where the training college used to be, because he's in trouble and I've got to help him?'"

"Yes, and when I told her all about what had happened, Leonora took me there," said April. "It's posh apartments now, but we snooped around and there's an underground parking garage. Leonora pretended that she was lost and had to sit down and that Pluto was thirsty. The attendant was helpful, and they got into this fantastic conversation about what Beeton was like in the old days, and the attendant said, 'You won't believe it, but behind the old generator at the end of this garage, there's supposed to be a tunnel that goes all the way to the center of town,' and then *I* said—'*Oh!*'"

The light in the shelter was suddenly half as bright as before.

"Oh, not yours *too*," said Stuart irritably.

"What's the matter?" asked Leonora.

"Her flashlight battery's dying."

"Then we'd better hurry," replied Leonora. "Pluto's a guide dog, not a guide mole. He needs a little bit of light or he can't see where he's going."

Pluto wagged his tail at the mention of his name and stood up eagerly.

"Are we going back to Great-Uncle Tony's workshop?" asked Stuart.

"Of *course* we are," said April. "Anyway, it's *your* workshop now, isn't it?"

"Try telling Jeannie that," said Stuart, but he felt invigorated: the combination of potato chips and company was very cheering. It was good to be part of a team, even if one member was blind, and one was a bit short, and one was a dog.

"Is everyone ready?" asked Leonora in a teacherish voice. "Then off we go."

By the time they had walked back to the workshop entrance, April's flashlight was about as much use as a luminous watch dial. Stuart had to feel around the edges of the door to confirm that it was still closed. He gave the springs at the bottom a fruitless tug. "So, what do we do now?" he asked.

"The Horten Ready Release," said Leonora.

"The what?"

"Every sealed cabinet that Tony made had a safety catch. It meant that Lily could open it if there was a problem. Feel around behind the springs. There should be a little knob on both sides."

There was.

"Now push them away from each other."

There was a quiet *click*, and the back of the cabinet lifted silently, like a car hood. Stuart found himself looking directly into the workshop through the open front cover of the book. And staring straight back at him was the round, hamsterish face of Clifford.

CHAPTER 31

"Oh!" said Clifford. "Er . . ."

There was a camera slung around his neck, and he was holding a pen and a notepad. Behind him, the late-afternoon sun was slanting through the opening in the ceiling and everything in the workshop was bathed in golden light, including a solid-looking fireman's ladder that now bridged the gap between the bandstand floor and the outside world. There was no one else in sight.

"Hello, Clifford," said Stuart brazenly. "Can I come in?" Without waiting for an answer, he climbed through the book cabinet and then turned to help Leonora.

"Thank you so much," she said graciously. She had unclipped Pluto from his harness, and the dog jumped neatly over the threshold, closely followed by April.

"Er . . ." said Clifford again, his eyes darting between them. "I'd better go and tell Jeannie. She's talking to a newspaper about selling the pictures," and he turned and began to hurry toward the fireman's ladder.

"Don't!" said Leonora. Her voice wasn't loud, but there was a calm authority to it, and Clifford hesitated and looked back.

"All we want is a little time in here," said Leonora. "What harm could we possibly do?"

Clifford puffed out his cheeks, undecided, and then he glanced toward the ladder again. The white dove was perched near the top of it, preening its feathers.

"I'm supposed to be guarding the place as well as cataloguing," he said. "Jeannie's made it a grade-two requirement. She says I'm within a whisker of the top mark."

"She'll never let you pass that exam," said Leonora.

Clifford stared at her. "What?"

"Jeannie will never let you pass Grade Two Basic Magic Skills," repeated Leonora slowly. "She will keep on failing you until your savings run out, and then she will get rid of you and take on another student who, like yourself, has spent his whole life longing to be a magician. She doesn't care about your ambition. She simply wants your cash."

Clifford's hands gripped the clipboard. "But she told me I had genuine talent," he said in a hoarse voice.

"And perhaps you have," replied Leonora. "But you'll never find out while she's using you as an unpaid servant. I think that she was once truly interested in stage magic, but I have heard the change in her over the years, and now all she thinks about is money and power. For Jeannie, this place isn't a house of wonders, it's a checkbook. Her road isn't your road, Clifford. You must find your own way."

There was silence for a moment. The dove clattered its wings, and settled on a lower rung.

"Tony Horten cared about magic," said Leonora.

"Will you show me around his workshop? Will you describe for me what you can see?"

She held out a hand, and after a moment Clifford came toward her. His face had lost some of its eager silliness. He smiled a little sadly, and linked his arm in hers.

"The Pharaoh's Cabinet," he said, leading her away toward the pyramid. "Five sides and at least ten doors, all of which fold in on themselves . . ."

Stuart let out the breath that he realized he'd been holding.

"Wow!" said April. "She's *good*. So what do we do now?"

Stuart gaped at her.

"I know." She smiled. "I normally do the telling, not the asking. But it's your workshop."

Stuart put a hand in his pocket and felt for the coins again. They seemed to burn in his palm.

"I could make a wish," he said. *To be taller*, he thought. He could do it. This time, he could really do it. His mouth was dry.

"But will it work?" she asked. "Is the magic for real?"

"Oh, yes," said Stuart. He could still feel the tug of it.

He walked over to the well, and after a moment April joined him. "What if something goes wrong?" she asked. "What if you can't get back again, like your uncle?"

Stuart took the threepences out of his pocket and clenched his hand around them.

"What would I tell your parents?" asked April.

He could feel himself trembling. He swallowed and took a deep breath.

"Don't," said April. "Don't go."

There was a nudge on the back of Stuart's leg. He looked down to see Pluto sniffing around, and behind him were Clifford and Leonora.

". . . And this is the Well of Wishes," Clifford was saying, and Leonora stepped forward, quickly reaching out her hands. She touched the parapet, at first tentatively, and then with a fierce grip.

"It's a bit hard to describe," continued Clifford. "I don't know how it was made, but there's an odd sort of shimmer to it . . ."

Leonora gazed down. Her face was patterned

with light and her eyes seemed to be searching for someone who wasn't there. She looked both happy and infinitely sad. "Lily," she said very quietly. "Where are you?"

Slowly, slowly, Stuart unclenched his palm.

He looked at what was in it—one coin bent, the other perfect—and then he touched Leonora's arm. "Here," he said, slipping the undamaged threepence into her hand. "Take this."

She lifted her head and fingered the coin.

"No," she said. "No, that's yours."

He shook his head. "It's yours now."

"And anyway, he's got another one," said April, butting in.

Stuart shot her an irritated look. "Take it," he insisted, turning back to Leonora. "Please. It's for you to wish with."

She hesitated for a moment, and then she smiled, a huge smile, so that she looked suddenly like a young woman. She reached down and slipped a hand under Pluto's collar. "I want to be with Lily and Tony again," she said quickly, and she held up her other hand and dropped the coin into the well. But it didn't fall. It hung in the air, spinning—spinning so fast that it looked like a tiny brass sphere, a miniature planet, a shining new world. And as it spun, it shone more and more brightly, until it was just a brilliant flicker.

Leonora waited, the light stroking her face. The air all around her and Pluto seemed to ripple. And then, as swiftly as if a curtain had been drawn across them, they disappeared.

The brilliant light blinked off. The workshop was suddenly darker.

Stuart and April and Clifford stood like a row of waxworks, scarcely breathing.

For a long minute there was utter silence and then from behind them someone spoke. "What. Was. *That?*"

Stuart turned stiffly and saw Jeannie halfway down the ladder.

"What was THAT?" She shouted the last word, her face white with disbelief, and she started to climb down again, but clumsily, as if she couldn't remember where her feet were.

Stuart felt his arm being pulled. "Let's go," said

April. "I don't like this. It's scaring me."

He couldn't seem to move.

She pulled at him again. "Let's get out of here. Stuart! Come *on*."

He nodded stiffly and at last managed to unglue his feet from the floor. But Jeannie had already reached them and she grabbed Stuart by the neck of his T-shirt and pushed him against the parapet of the well.

"*Tell me what I have just seen,*" she demanded.

"Get OFF him!" shouted April.

Jeannie swatted her away like a moth. "Where did Leonora go?" she asked, with each word giving Stuart a shake, and with the other hand fending off a yelling April. "Tell me!"

"I don't know," said Stuart between gasps.

"TELL ME!"

"The same place that Great-Uncle Tony went."

"And where was that?" she demanded, her face pushed close to Stuart's. His head was over the parapet of the well, one arm bent behind him, the other pinned at the wrist by Jeannie's elbow. "I want to know."

258

"That's enough!" said Clifford, and his voice was so bullish that for a moment Jeannie actually did stop, midshake.

"What did you say?" she asked incredulously, her hand still gripping Stuart's T-shirt.

"I said ... er ... *That's enough*," repeated Clifford, sounding less like a bull and more like a sheep.

"If," said Jeannie coldly, "you wish to pass Grade Two Basic Magic Skills, then one of the first requirements is cooperation with your tutor."

Clifford's whole face seemed to wobble with indecision, and then all at once it set, quite firmly. "I don't care," he said.

Jeannie's grip on Stuart's collar became even tighter. "What?" she asked.

"I don't care," repeated Clifford. "Let him go."

"Yes, let him go!" shouted April, dragging on Jeannie's arm, and receiving a shove that made her stagger backward and fall over her own feet.

"If you think—" began Jeannie, then she ducked as something white skimmed her head. It was the dove, wheeling around and then settling, with a flurry of wing-beats, on Clifford's shoulder. And in that second, Jeannie's grip on Stuart loosened, and he started to struggle away. She caught him again by the shoulders, squeezing hard. "Where did Tony Horten disappear to?" she shouted.

"I wish I knew," said Stuart hoarsely.

He tried to twist out of her grasp and his wrist hit the parapet of the well. His hand jerked open. The threepence, the last threepence, seemed to trickle into the air. It hung there; a little crooked moon.

And April, sprawled on the floor, saw Stuart and Jeannie dissolve in a blaze of pale light.

Stuart found himself in flickering darkness, in the middle of a whirlwind, pulled and buffeted, twisted and punched, the only noise a distorted roar. Then distantly, through the roar, he heard a voice—the voice of a young woman, brisk and light.

"*I'm sick of this dreary old war,*" she said. "*I wish I could go back to a time before bombs and sirens.*"

The flickering slowed and settled, the buffeting ceased, the world turned from shadow to substance. Another voice detached itself from the roar.

"Ladies and gentlemen, the Great Hortini and his lovely wife will now demonstrate the Cabinet of Curious Change, a wondrous and extraordinary mechanism, indeed!"

And suddenly Stuart could see again, but everything looked strange and distant, as if he were peering through thickened glass.

He was in a vast theater, sitting on a red plush seat, looking up at a stage that was lit by a row of dancing flames. On the stage, a short, vigorous gray-haired man with a very large mustache and a scarlet waistcoat was standing, with one hand outstretched.

A red-haired woman all dressed in gold and scarlet stepped to his side, smiling.

"The Cabinet of Curious Change!" she announced, and whipped away a length of silk that was covering a large object. It was revealed to be an elaborate cabinet, decorated with silver filigree and bright enamel. She opened the door to show the empty interior, closed it again, and then revolved the whole cabinet. It turned smoothly, the sides and back glittering with gold leaf.

"And now," she said, "the Great Hortini requires a volunteer from the audience!"

Stuart looked around, and the world swum in and out of focus. It was like being in the depths of a dream and yet he could feel the seat beneath him, could smell the gaslight, could hear the murmur of the audience, and see the flutter of the ladies' fans. No one was raising a hand.

"A volunteer is required!" repeated the Great Hortini. He stepped to the front of the stage. "And are there none?" he asked. "Are you all, perhaps, just a little afraid of change?"

He smiled, and a chuckle swept across the audience. "Then I shall have to choose someone." His eyes swept across the rows. "You there," he said, pointing directly at Stuart. "The lad in the blue trousers. Come onto the stage, if you will."

There was a scatter of applause, and Stuart found himself on his feet and moving like a sleepwalker along the aisle and up the steps that led up to the stage. The Great Hortini nodded at him and then addressed the audience once again.

"The Cabinet of Curious Change, ladies and

gentlemen, is a wonder of our age, a simple container that can utterly transform its contents. We have here an ordinary boy—" He placed a hand on Stuart's shoulder and glanced down at him.

"Your name, my lad," he asked.

"Stuart Horten," said Stuart. And the Great Hortini's expression changed to one of incredulity.

And in that instant the world seemed to snap into focus, clear and sharp, bright and real, and Stuart knew that he was actually *there*, not dreaming, not hallucinating, but standing on the stage of a theater a hundred years or more before he was born.

A hush fell.

The Great Hortini knelt on one knee so that he was on Stuart's level. "Not an ordinary boy at all," he said very quietly. "An exceptional boy. *The right sort of boy*. You're the one who found my note, aren't you?"

"Your note?"

"That I left in the tin: *My workshop and all it contains is yours it you can find it . . .*"

"I found the note," said Stuart. "And I found the workshop."

"Then you're the right sort of boy to have it." He nodded gravely. "Well done, Stuart."

"So you mean *you're* my great-uncle? You're Teeny-Tiny Tony Horten?"

"I was once. And then I followed my Lily into the world that she'd wished for, a world before sirens and bombs. And in this older world I needed a new name. I became the Great Hortini, the wonder of the Victorian stage, but the Great Hortini is, and always was, and always shall be, Tony Horten."

He paused, and in the moment of silence Stuart realized that there was not a whisper from the audience, not a hiss from the gas-burners, not a creak from the stage. More than that, there was no movement—the audience sat like wooden dummies, the flames looked like a row of folded orange napkins.

"What's happening?" asked Stuart. He moved his shoulders uneasily; he could feel a pressure on them as if they were being gripped.

The Great Hortini stood and looked around, his expression sharp and quizzical. "You used a threepence to get here?" he asked.

"The very last one. It was damaged, though, bent right across the middle. And I made a sort of accidental wish."

"What was it?"

"That I'd know where you'd disappeared to."

The pressure on his shoulders was increasing. It was as if he could still feel Jeannie's hands.

"What's happening?" he asked again, staring at the frozen faces in the audience,

"I think I know," said the Great Hortini. "Imagine if you threw a stone into the air—it would travel upward, hang for a split second, and then fall. The imperfect coin, the last threepence, slung you into the past and this is the briefest of pauses before you begin your return journey. You could say that for a single moment, we are outside time." He smiled and held out his hand. "It has been an honor to meet you, young man. A great and unexpected honor. You brought Leonora back to us, and we shall always, always be grateful. She describes you as a fellow of great pluck and resourcefulness, and I can see that she is right. Enjoy the workshop. It has many surprises."

Stuart shook his hand, and as he did so the air seemed to stir, as if ruffled by a breeze.

Someone in the audience coughed, someone else rustled a program, the flames leaped and trembled, and the theater was suddenly alive again.

"And now, ladies and gentlemen," announced the Great Hortini, moving seamlessly back into his role as performer, "my lovely wife, Lily, will escort this young fellow into the Cabinet of Curious Change."

Stuart felt his hand being taken and he looked up to see Lily smiling down at him. He tried to smile back but the invisible hold on his shoulders was growing painful now, and the world was becoming dreamlike again. He stepped into the cabinet, turned around, and saw the door close on him.

In the darkness Great-Uncle Tony's voice was still quite audible: ". . . we shall now revolve the Cabinet of Curious Change three times in a clockwise direction . . ."

The floor began to twist under Stuart's feet and he placed his hands on the walls to steady himself. He could feel the hurricane beginning again, the same one that had dragged him into the past.

". . . and now we shall revolve the cabinet in the reverse direction three times. You see, ladies and gentlemen that there are no hidden compartments, no wires, no trap doors . . ."

As the magical wind tore and tugged at Stuart, the grip on his shoulders loosened and then broke, and he felt himself being whirled into the storm. He was no longer in the darkness of the cabinet but flying above the heads of the audience, staring down at the stage. The scene seemed to shudder before his eyes like a faulty film.

"The curious change is complete!" announced the Great Hortini. "Let us see how our young volunteer has fared."

Lily stepped forward and opened the door, and before the flickering darkness once again engulfed Stuart, he saw that the cabinet wasn't empty. Someone was standing inside it, someone that he recognized.

It was Jeannie. And she looked absolutely *furious*.

In the room beneath the bandstand, April scrambled to her feet and stared open-mouthed at the empty space beside the Well of Wishes, where, just a second earlier, Stuart and Jeannie had been standing.

"But—" she said.

Clifford, the dove still cooing on his shoulder, took a step forward. "Where—?" he asked.

"*OW!*" yelled Stuart, crashing to the floor out of nowhere. "That hurt!" he remarked, rubbing his hip, and then looked up to see two dazed faces looking down at him.

"Where have you come from?" asked April.

"Where did you go to?" asked Clifford.

Stuart shook his head, still full of the thunder of the journey.

"And where's Jeannie?" added Clifford.

"It's a long story," said Stuart, getting up slowly. "A very long story."

Before he could say more, there was noise behind them—a clatter of footsteps on the fireman's ladder—and they all turned to see a man climbing down. He had a keen expression and a camera slung over his shoulder.

"Well, *wow!*" he said, jumping the last two rungs to the floor and looking around. "This is *incredible*!

I'm Dave Harper, incidentally, from the *East Midlands Gazette*, I was just talking to the mayoress earlier. Where is she?"

Clifford and April looked at Stuart.

He thought hard. "Meeting new people," he said.

"Oh, right." Dave Harper raised his camera and snapped a couple of photos of the Well of Wishes. "Well, she was being very mysterious about what was down here. Don't suppose you can tell me anything about it?"

Stuart took a deep breath. "It was the workshop of Tony Horten, a magician often known by his stage name of Teeny-Tiny Tony Horten. He started his stage career in the nineteen-thirties, and he designed and built all his own illusions, inspired by the famous Victorian stage engineers, such as the Great Hortini, whose real name was also Horten. He was the inventor of the Horten Ready-Release, a safety catch used on many of his greatest illusions, including the Book of Peril which you can see over there to your right."

Dave Harper glanced at the giant book and then looked back at Stuart, his expression baffled.

"But how do know all that?" he asked. "How do you know so much about this workshop?"

Stuart grinned.

The answer was simple and wonderful and true.

"Because it's mine," he said.

THE END

BIRMINGHAM GAZETTE

1883

STARTLING APPOINTMENT OF LADY

The New Birmingham Magic Trick Factory has caused much consternation in the manufacturing community by appointing a lady to the post of Manager. "I was deeply shocked when she applied for the position," said the owner, Amos Sithfield. "But her knowledge and skills were undeniably far superior to those of the other applicants. She has recently moved to this country, she says, and has acquired her experience elsewhere."

The lady in question, Miss Jean Carr, declined to comment and, indeed, attacked this reporter with her umbrella when he attempted to interview her. He can, however, confirm that she has a good loud voice, and a commanding manner.

The reporter wishes the best of luck to her future workforce.